Peyton wasn't sure what to do.

This was one of those awkward moments at the end of the evening, so she said, "I had a lovely evening," and leaned in for a hug and a quick peck, but Malik changed the momentum by turning his head, so her kiss landed on his lips instead of his cheek.

Peyton was stunned at first—she hadn't expected that—but she didn't stop him either. The caress of his lips on her mouth set her aflame with desire. And when Malik took it a step further and deepened the kiss, invading her mouth with his tongue, Peyton moaned.

As the kiss became more passionate, Malik folded Peyton in his arms and pulled her firmly to him. He loved the taste of her and the feel of her breasts against his chest. His pulse raced as his hands dipped and settled firmly on her hips. Malik felt the hardness in his pants press up against Peyton. Carried away by his own response, he didn't even notice Peyton resisting until she had pushed him away.

Books by Yahrah St. John

Kimani Romance

Never Say Never
Risky Business of Love
Playing for Keeps
This Time for Real

Kimani Arabesque

One Magic Moment
Dare to Love

YAHRAH ST. JOHN

lives in Orlando, the City Beautiful, but was born in the Windy City, Chicago. A graduate of Hyde Park Career Academy, she earned a bachelor of arts degree in English from Northwestern University.

St. John began writing at the age of twelve, and to date has written more than twenty short stories and published six novels. Her books have garnered four-star ratings from *Romantic Times BOOKReviews,* Rawsistaz Reviewers, Romance in Color and numerous book clubs. A member of Romance Writers of America, St. John is an avid reader of all genres. She enjoys the arts, cooking, travel and adventure sports, but her true passion remains writing.

THIS TIME
for REAL

YAHRAH ST. JOHN

KIMANI
ROMANCE

This book is dedicated to my father and champion,
Austin Mitchell.

An enormous thank-you to all my family, friends and
loyal readers for their continued support.
I couldn't do it without you.

KIMANI PRESS™

ISBN-13: 978-0-373-86102-6
ISBN-10:   0-373-86102-8

Recycling programs
for this product may
not exist in your area.

THIS TIME FOR REAL

Copyright © 2009 by Yahrah Yisrael

www.kimanipress.com

Printed in U.S.A.

Dear Reader,

What an exciting ride it was writing *This Time for Real*.
I felt Malik Williams's story was the next logical one for
the Orphan series as he was so outspoken in the first
installment, *Playing for Keeps*. I wanted to share with you
how a cynical crusader like Malik could heal the wounds
of his traumatic past while finding love where he least
expected it. Widowed professor Peyton Sawyer was not
only the perfect blend of beauty and intellect, but she
easily matched wills with stubborn Malik. Her steely
determination in refusing to give up on him until he let
love in was poignant. It also gave me an opportunity to
catch up with old friends Quentin and Avery while setting
the stage for feisty Sage Anderson as our next heroine. I
hope you enjoyed the read and I look forward to bringing
you more sexy love stories.

I love hearing from fans, so please feel free to drop me a
note at yahrah@yahrahstjohn.com. Also be sure to visit
my Web site at www.yahrahstjohn.com for the latest
contests and book signings in your area.

All the best,

Yahrah St. John

Chapter 1

"Welcome to New York, sis." Jude Allen gave his big sister Peyton Sawyer a long hug as he entered her one-bedroom apartment in Brooklyn.

He stood and assessed his sister. Although he hadn't seen her in several months, Peyton looked as beautiful as ever, fit and trim in a fuchsia track suit. Her warm cocoa-colored skin glowed and her shoulder-length black hair shone brightly. His big sister was a real looker. Jude was going to have to beat the New York fellas away with a stick.

"Thanks," Peyton said, smiling warmly and pulling him inside. "Make yourself at home. That's if you can find a place to sit." Boxes filled up nearly every square inch.

"I'm so glad you're here," Jude said. "Now I don't feel so alone. I have family in town."

"Not that you need me," Peyton commented. Her

baby brother was an extrovert and made friends easily. She couldn't wait to see Jude the actor in action. He'd already acquired a bit part on a soap opera and was hoping to snag a Broadway show.

"No regrets?" he asked, pushing several boxes aside and sitting on her leather sofa. She'd sure surprised the heck out of him and their parents when she'd left her professorship at Cleveland State University to move to New York.

"None." Peyton shook her head. "I needed to make a change," she replied. "And what better way than to come to New York, right?" She felt she didn't have to say what she really felt, which was that after losing her husband David Sawyer in a terrible three-car pile up five years ago, she was ready for a change of scenery.

"I understand." Jude patted her knee. Cleveland held too many memories. "You can get lost here."

"Exactly."

"But neither Amber nor I will let you do that," Jude replied. "We're here to keep you centered."

Peyton smiled. Amber Martin was her dear friend from college. They'd kept in touch over the years since finishing their PhDs and now they would be teaching at New York University together. "And I appreciate that. But I've got my work cut out for me. Making tenure is not going to be easy." The Dean of the College of Education fully expected her to publish several articles a year before making tenure.

"True, but no one is more driven than you," Jude said. "You'll make tenure." Peyton had known she wanted to teach for as long as he could remember. When they were younger, she'd follow their mom and sit in on her classes while Jude on the other hand preferred the arts. He supposed he got that from his father, who was a musician.

"From your lips to God's ears," Peyton said, laughing.

"You don't need divine intervention," Jude replied. "If had to put my money on anyone, I'd put it on you every time."

"We need funding, Malik. The center needs to be painted," Theresa Harris commented. "And the computer center needs new printers."

"Don't you think I know all of this?" Malik asked, exasperation in his voice. As director, he was aware of all facets that went into keeping the center's medical and recreational facilities in tip-top condition. He'd been the director of the Harlem Community Center since his mentor Andrew Webster had retired and handed the reigns over to him five years ago. Given his success at HCC, he'd recently been given the added responsibility of overseeing several centers throughout Manhattan, but he kept HCC as his home base.

The promotion had increased not only his workload, but his paycheck as well. Malik was doing quite well for himself and owned a renovated brownstone in Harlem. He'd been smart to buy many years ago when no one would have been caught dead living in Central Harlem. Now his brownstone was worth over a million dollars. Who would have ever thought that he, an orphan since the age of ten, would have what he had?

"I have a meeting coming up with the Community Advisory Board at Children's Aid Network. But what we really need is a corporate sponsor. In the meantime, however, we'll have to make do."

"And did I mention we need another volunteer doctor?" Theresa added.

"Now *that,* I have a handle on," Malik replied, shifting through the manila folders on his desk. He'd already interviewed several doctors who'd offered to come in one day a week to ease the load in the health clinic. "I have several candidates, and it's just a process of picking the best one." Malik didn't know what he'd do without his right hand. As assistant director of the Harlem Community Center, Theresa kept Malik focused. "But I appreciate you bringing it all to my attention."

"And now that we have business covered, what are we going to do about your love life?" she asked. Over six feet tall, Malik Williams was a fine-looking man. Even with long dreads and a permanent five o'clock shadow, a black Bob Marley T-shirt and some faded blue jeans, Malik exuded a raw masculinity. Theresa didn't know why he was still single.

"I appreciate the concern," Malik replied, "but I'm not interested in seeing anyone right now. My plate is full."

"Do you even remember the last time you had a date?" Theresa asked. "Because I sure can't. You need to find you a good woman to settle down with. I know you'd make an excellent husband and father. I see the way you interact with those kids as their basketball coach."

"Theresa," he said with exaggerated patience, "Marriage isn't for me." He'd seen what marriage could do to people. How it made you lose all common sense and not realize that the man you'd brought into the fold as father to your son was beating the crap out of him. Malik would never forget what it was like being on the receiving end of his stepfather, Joe Johnson's belt. It was better he left marriage to all the gullible people in the world. The ones who believed that love could conquer all instead of the reality that love was blind.

"How would you know?" Theresa responded. "You've never been in a relationship long enough to find out."

"I get what I need."

Theresa didn't blink at Malik's comment. "If you're referring to sex, there's more to a relationship."

"I am. And sex is all I need. Both parties get mutual satisfaction without all the entanglements. Trust me, Theresa. I'm better off." Malik closed the folder. "Now if you'll excuse me, I do have some place I need to be."

Malik glanced at his watch. He was already late for dinner with his best friends, Dante Moore, Sage Anderson and Quentin Davis. The foursome had grown up together at the orphanage, but despite their rocky start they'd all gone on to have successful careers. Dante owned his own restaurant, Sage was a corporate attorney and Quentin was a world-renowned photographer. But this spring their tight family unit had been put to the test with some major drama and they'd all vowed to never let anything come between them again.

Theresa had been his assistant the last five years and knew when he was brushing her off. "Tell Sage, Dante and Q, I said hello."

Malik turned at the door and glanced at her. She knew him too darn well. "Sure thing, Theresa. I'll see you tomorrow."

"I can't believe we're going to be working together," Amber commented as she helped Peyton unpack her new office.

"I'm excited too." Peyton smiled at her best friend. "You just don't know how much I needed a change." She loaded her arms up with books and placed them on the bookshelves from the previous professor.

"I think I have some idea," Amber replied. "Here, let me help you with that." Amber took several books out of Peyton's arms. "So, have you had the opportunity to meet some of the department faculty?"

"Briefly, at a faculty brunch during the interview process in May; but I haven't seen anyone yet. I can't believe it's already August and fall semester starts in a week."

Amber watched as Peyton put every book in alphabetical order according to title. Peyton hated things out of place. "I'm sure they'll pop by and stick their heads in. They can't resist getting the scoop on new blood." Amber chuckled. "We professors are such gossips."

"I'll have to remember that," Peyton replied. "And make sure my skeletons stay hidden."

"As if you had any." Amber laughed derisively. "You are the most straightlaced person I know."

"And you are the most radical," Peyton replied, turning around and staring at her hippie friend. In all the years they'd known each other, Amber hadn't changed a bit, except for maybe the hair. The hair was shorter in a chic layer bob, but her style was still the same. Wearing hiphuggers, a novelty T-shirt and a pageboy cap, Amber looked like a student, instead of an accomplished professor with a PhD in women's studies.

"True, and that's why we make a great team. You are going to have so much fun in New York. Cleveland will be a distant memory."

"What's our first step?"

"First we're going to get you settled in," Amber began, "and then we'll hit the New York dating scene."

"I don't know about all that," Peyton replied. They weren't the ladies of *Sex and the City.* Peyton wasn't ready for an active social life. She'd been on a few dates the last couple of years, but she'd felt so guilty. David had been the only man she'd ever loved. They'd known each other since they were in kindergarten, and when she'd matured into womanhood love had blossomed. It was hard for her not to compare every man she met to David, as if it would even be possible for them to live up to such a high standard.

"Don't you trust me?" Amber asked, giving Peyton her most innocent face.

Famous last words, thought Peyton.

Malik strolled into Dante's tapas bar half an hour later than expected, and Sage wasted no time.

"You're late," Sage commented, looking down at her watch when Malik joined her at the wave-shaped bar.

"I'm sorry. I had several things to attend to," Malik answered the beautiful, brown-skinned, five-foot, three-inch barracuda of a lawyer who also happened to be one of his dear friends.

"More important than us?" Sage countered.

"Don't answer that." Dante pointed his finger at Malik from behind the bar. "Not if you know what's good for you." He returned to making several drinks for patrons. Even though he was working, Dante always managed to look casually put together in slacks and a crew neck sweater.

"Well, from the looks of it—" Malik glanced around the nearly full restaurant "—I am not the only one." He didn't see Quentin or his girlfriend Avery Roberts anywhere.

"Quentin had the courtesy to call," Sage replied.

"You mean the Quentin Davis who can do no wrong in your eyes, you mean *that* Quentin?" Malik pinched Sage's nose as he took the barstool next to her.

"Stop that." Sage patted away his hand. Malik used to do it all the time when they were growing up at the orphanage together. That's when he wasn't fighting off the bullies that made fun of her constant sickliness. Back then she'd suffered from terrible allergies, not to mention her asthma, which had gone undetected due to her mother's drug use and neglect.

"Greetings!" Quentin walked in with his girlfriend Avery. Malik had to admit that if anyone had ever told him there would come a day in which a player like Quentin would be settling down with one woman, he would have called them crazy. But he couldn't knock Quentin, because he had never seen him happier.

"Good to see you, bro." Malik rose from the stool and patted him on the back. "Avery." He kissed her on the cheek. "You're looking well." Not that Malik had ever seen Avery's razor-cut, shoulder-length hair out of place. Fair in comparison to Quentin's chocolate complexion, Avery was class and sophistication all rolled into one.

"Thank you." Avery smiled back.

"So what's on the menu tonight, Dante?" Malik asked. He liked that they'd all incorporated a weekly dinner into their daily lives. When Quentin had been photographing the war in Iraq, a part of their foursome was missing and dinner hadn't been the same.

"A little of this, a little of that," Dante replied coyly. He always liked to surprise the group with new recipes. "What can I get the two of you to drink?" he asked Quentin and Avery.

"A Heineken and a glass of pinot grigio, please."

"How's the center?" Sage inquired.

"Busy and fast-paced," Malik replied. There was always paperwork to complete or a meeting to attend about funding, programming, etc. "Truth be told, the center is in dire need of a renovation."

"I couldn't agree with you more," Quentin replied. Since he'd begun mentoring the center's youth in photography, Quentin had seen the work that needed to be done.

"Have you brought this up to Children's Aid Network?" Avery inquired. Avery was very familiar with charitable organizations, since her mother was one of their biggest supporters.

"I plan on it, but it's a tough position for CAN. They have to weigh which program or center needs the money the most. And HCC has to fall in line just like everyone else."

"Sounds like you need a corporate sponsor," Sage replied.

"That would be a dream come true. A benefactor completely focused on just the Harlem center," Malik replied.

"I'll ask around," Avery piped in. With her parent's social standing in the community, she was exposed to many influential people—but only one immediately sprang to mind.

Quentin noticed the grin on Avery's face and whispered in her ear. "You have someone in mind, don't you?"

Avery nodded. "I do and I'll tell you all about it later."

"How's the law firm?" Malik asked, changing the subject. As much as he loved the center, he needed a break from worrying about its troubles.

"Well, I feel like I can see the end of the road," Sage replied. "I've been at the firm for four and a half years. I'm hoping I can make partner in five."

"Don't kill yourself trying."

"Oh please, Malik," Sage chuckled. "You are just as bad as I am. You spend your whole life at that center."

"This is true," Quentin said, coming over with his Heineken.

"I'm dedicated." Malik defended himself.

"To your work," Dante finished.

"And what's wrong with that?"

"You need to find some time for romance, my friend,"

Quentin pulled Avery towards him and planted a swift kiss on her lips.

"Like you?" Malik said, smiling. "Hmm, I think I'll leave you to that love stuff. I don't believe in love." Malik had seen the flipside of the love coin. Everyday at the center, he saw men who beat their wives, men who left their wives, wives who abandoned their children for men. Love? Love he could do without.

"You are a true cynic, my friend," Quentin replied. He too, had been a cynic, but Avery had changed all of that for him. Now he was love's biggest advocate. "But just you wait when that love bug hits you. Trust me, you won't know what to do."

"It's never going to happen." For Malik, the only thing a woman was good for was the short term.

After they'd unpacked her office, Peyton and Amber headed over to a restaurant Amber suggested in the Village. "You'll love this place," Amber said on the walk over to Dante's. "They make the best tapas I've ever had. And since you're such a light eater, you'll love it. And there's usually a good crowd on Friday night, so we can mingle."

"I'm your guinea pig," Peyton said, following her inside.

The décor was upscale and chic, with dark red, mustard and orange shades. It had a circular wave bar and small intimate booths and tables throughout. The soft lighting was just enough for you to see your companion across the table. "I like, I like," Peyton said.

A hostess greeted them and led them to a booth across from a large table for six. Peyton noticed that an attractive fellow with dreads was checking her out as she approached.

"Did you see that guy?" Peyton asked, once they were seated.

"Which one?" Amber asked, glancing at the table. She saw three attractive-looking brothers, two of whom looked like they had dates. Which meant that only one was available.

"The one in the dreads." When Amber turned around to look, Peyton reached across the table and grabbed her arm. "Don't look."

"Why not?" Amber threw a furtive glance their way. "Oh yes, he's hot," she commented. "But I wouldn't think you'd go for his type. He's much more *my* speed."

Amber was right. Usually, Peyton liked her men clean-cut, but there was something about this one that appealed to her. She'd felt a stirring as soon as her eyes made contact with his. She'd never felt such an instant spark with someone before and it disturbed her. "You can have him," Peyton replied tersely. "As I stated before, I'm not ready to date."

"Will you ever be?" Amber wondered aloud. "Eventually, you've got to get back on the horse. It's been five long years, Peyton. You're a relatively young woman and you have your whole life ahead of you."

Peyton sighed. "I know, but it's easier said than done."

"Did you conjure her up?" Malik asked, turning to Sage.

How else to explain the beautiful creature—with the jet-black hair that hung luxuriously to her shoulders, deep-set brown eyes and flawless skin—that had just crossed his line of vision?

"Who?"

"The beautiful brunette who just walked in with the hippie," Malik answered.

Sage glanced around and her eyes landed on the booth across from them. "I thought you were immune to the fairer sex?"

"What I am is human," Malik stated.

"She *is* a stunner," Dante commented from his side.

"I'll say," Quentin added. When Avery glanced in his direction, Quentin recanted. "But no one is as beautiful as you, my love."

"That's what you'd better say." Avery chuckled. She wasn't worried about Quentin's former playboy ways. She knew he was a reformed man.

"Do you want to meet her?" Dante asked.

"Yeah, I do."

"C'mon," Dante stood. "Their drinks are coming. I'll go introduce myself as the owner and that'll be your cue."

"Thanks." Malik quickly followed behind him. When they arrived at the table, all conversation ceased and the two women looked up from their sangrias.

"Ladies," Dante began. "How are you this evening?"

"Well, thank you," Amber replied.

"I'm Dante. The owner." He extended his hand to Amber and then to Peyton.

"It's a pleasure," Amber batted her eyelashes at him. Dante was a fine-looking man, and she hoped he was available. "I've been here a few times and the tapas have been divine."

"Thanks, I appreciate that." Dante beamed with pride.

From his side, Malik only had eyes for one woman, but the brunette seemed to be trying her best to avoid looking at him.

"And this here is Malik Williams." Dante motioned him over.

"Sistas," Malik said, smiling at the ladies.

Peyton merely nodded while Amber extended her

hand. "I'm Amber Martin and this is my friend Peyton Sawyer. We're both professors at NYU, so you might be seeing us here often."

"That's my alma mater," Malik replied, shaking her hand. He'd received his masters in Business Administration at NYU.

"Small world." Amber kicked Peyton underneath the table. Here was a gorgeous fox standing in front of them and she was acting like a bump on a log.

"Why don't you join us at my table?" Dante encouraged the duo. "We've got plenty, and I'm sure there are a few tapas you haven't tried before, Amber."

Malik had to hand it to Dante, he was smooth. Inviting the women to join them was smooth and would give them time to get better acquainted.

"We would love to." Amber jumped up from the table and grabbed her sangria glass.

Peyton glared at Amber. She loved her friend to pieces, but she didn't appreciate being kidnapped.

"Does your friend speak?" Malik inquired, grinning at Peyton because she hadn't said a word.

"Yes, I do," a quiet, but firm voice uttered from rose-tinted lips. When Peyton glanced up at him, she wished she hadn't. Malik Williams had skin the color of toffee and a sexy five o'clock shadow. Smoldering dark eyes met hers, eyes that Peyton could easily get lost in, forcing her to look down into her glass.

"And she would love to join you guys too, isn't that right, Peyton?" Amber gave her a look.

Peyton put on a polite smile. "Of course." When she rose from her chair, Malik rushed over to move it out of her way.

Malik allowed Peyton to precede him, giving him a nice view of her backside in the sexy jeans she wore.

Her figure was all the right proportions and she matched him in height. He estimated she was about five foot nine to his six foot one.

Although she couldn't see him, Peyton could feel Malik's eyes boring a hole through the back of her head as she walked ahead of him, and it made her nervous. She hadn't received such obvious male attention in some time.

"Everyone, I'd like to introduce you to Amber and Peyton," Dante said when they arrived at the table. "They'll be joining us for dinner. These are my friends Sage, Quentin and Avery."

Amber took the empty seat next to Dante while Malik grabbed a nearby chair for Peyton. He slid it under her with ease. "Thanks," Peyton said as she sat down. She tried not to lose her manners, even though she was extremely uncomfortable sitting so close to Malik.

"It was my pleasure," Malik replied.

"Peyton's new to town and I was just showing her around," Amber offered once they were seated.

"Perhaps I can help with that?" Malik replied eagerly, turning to Peyton. "I've lived here all my life and I'd be happy to show you around."

Sage smiled as she watched Malik. It had been a long time since she'd seen Malik so enthralled by a woman.

"That's really very nice of you…" Peyton struggled to remember his name, because he was staring at her like she was a cold glass of water after he'd come out of the scorching hot desert.

"Malik," he replied, refilling her sangria.

"Although I appreciate your offer, Malik," Peyton said, accepting the glass, "It really isn't necessary. I have Amber and my brother Jude."

"True, but you can never have too many friends," Malik answered. He tried not to let it bother him that

Peyton was rejecting his offer, but he couldn't help it, he was miffed. From the moment she'd walked in the door and he glanced her way, he'd felt his temperature rise. And the only way he was going to cool down was if he satisfied his curiosity.

The evening continued with Dante's waiters serving platters loaded with chicken croquettes, baked goat cheese with sweet onion marmalade, portabella mushrooms with herb dressing, spinach and artichokes on crostini and grilled sea scallops wrapped in proscuitto.

"This is way too much," Peyton commented. "There is no way we're going to eat all of this."

"You should try a little bit of everything," Malik commented from her side. "Dante's a master. Here try one." He picked up a spinach-and-artichoke crostini and offered it to her.

Peyton glanced across the table at Amber. Did he really expect her to let him feed her? It appeared so, because he and his friends were all staring at her and waiting.

"Go ahead," Dante encouraged her. "You'll love it."

Feeling pressured, Peyton opened her mouth and took a bite. Despite her best efforts, a moan escaped her lips. The small bite was so deliciously rich and creamy, she licked her lips.

Malik's groin tightened in response to her feminine moan. *Is that how she would sound if I were buried deep inside her?* "Want another?" he asked excitedly.

Due to Malik's tone, Peyton realized how blatantly sexual she must have sounded. All eyes at the table were on her. Peyton colored immediately and said, "No, thank you."

"It was that good, huh?" Quentin asked right before Avery kneed him.

"If it's that good, pass me the whole platter." Sage

laughed. She could use an orgasmic experience. Work had been extremely stressful of late.

"Me too," Amber piped in.

"Leave her be." Dante jumped into the fray. "There's plenty more where that came from." While he busied himself getting the platters moving around, Peyton lowered her head.

"Don't be embarrassed," Malik whispered so that only she could hear. "I liked your uninhibited response." Perhaps she was equally uninhibited in the bedroom. Malik sure hoped he'd have the opportunity to find out.

"Has anyone ever told you you're a flirt?"

"Guilty as charged," Malik said, grinning devilishly.

"Well, your charms won't work on me, Malik," Peyton huffed, then scooted her chair farther away.

"If you say so, but methinks the lady doth protest too much." Peyton was trying hard to act like she wasn't interested in him, but Malik didn't buy it for one second. He'd seen desire in her eyes when he'd fed her.

After the elaborate meal, good conversation, shared laughs and several more glasses of sangria, Peyton excused herself to go to the ladies' room. When she glanced at herself in the mirror, all she saw was fear. Fear of going forward, and fear of going back. Hadn't she come to New York for a fresh start? So why was that so difficult to do? Why was it so hard to allow a man like Malik to show interest in her? Peyton couldn't answer that question.

When she returned to the table and found Malik had gone, Peyton gave Amber a get-out-of-Dodge look, which, thankfully, her best friend heeded.

"Dante." Peyton came towards him and offered her hand. "Thank you for the lovely food, and to all of you." She waved at Sage, Quentin and Avery. "Thank you for sharing your evening with us. Good night."

"Good night, Peyton, Amber," several voices called out.

Peyton waved, grabbed Amber by the hand and flew out the door.

"You left without saying goodbye to Malik," Amber commented once they were outside. "He obviously liked you. What harm would it have been to let him take you around town and show you the sights?"

"The harm? The harm is…" Peyton's voice trailed off. She couldn't think of a single, logical reason she shouldn't go out with Malik, so she said, "I'm just too busy settling in. Can we please change the subject off men and to say…work?"

"All right," Amber conceded. You could bring a horse to water but you couldn't make them drink. "How can I help?"

"Well," Peyton thought quickly. "I'd like my students to complete some volunteer work along with my class, but I have no idea where to start."

"The SCA Internship Program has a lot of great volunteer jobs," Amber replied. "You should check out the listing in the department. They have a lot of opportunities in community centers and organizations throughout New York."

Relieved, Peyton squeezed Amber's arm. "Thanks, Amber. I think I'll do that."

Chapter 2

"We need new volunteers, Theresa. With several of our college interns returning to school after summer break, we are going to be short-staffed in the day care center." They needed interns to help the full-time staff with playtime, reading and dispensing breakfast and lunch. "How could you let this slip through the cracks?"

Theresa was irked by Malik's accusation. He knew how hard she worked. "What's your problem this morning?"

"Nothing," he replied tersely. "You just need to do your job."

"Now you listen here, Malik Williams." Theresa wagged her index finger at him. "I take a whole lot of crap off you because you have a lot on your shoulders, but I will not take you disrespecting me."

Instantly repentant, he apologized. "I'm sorry." He wasn't upset with Theresa. He was still smarting over the fact that the professor had rejected him. Peyton had captured Malik's attention immediately with her athletic figure and her attractive features, which had been devoid of makeup; but the professor had been determined to keep her distance, and that she had by skipping out without saying goodbye. "Really, I am." He squeezed Theresa's shoulder.

"All right, you're forgiven," she said reluctantly. "So what or *who* has gotten under your collar?"

"It doesn't matter." Malik shrugged, but that didn't stop his mind from wandering to Peyton's milk chocolate skin and long black hair that he'd love to run his fingers through.

"Yes, it does. When you come in breathing fire, it sure as hell does."

"What can I say?" Malik bunched his shoulders. "I met this beautiful woman on Friday night and she gave me the cold shoulder."

"So a *woman* has you this wound up. Who is she?"

"Her name is Peyton Sawyer and she's a professor at NYU."

"Speaking of," Theresa began. "NYU's education department has always been great with supplying volunteers for the center."

Malik nodded. She had a point. "Why don't you call and see if they have some candidates available? Of course, they'll have to apply and complete the physical and background check."

"I'm on it," Theresa said.

An hour later, Theresa had called over to the Metropolitan Studies Department and discovered that Professor Peyton Sawyer had expressed an interest in the center's volunteer program just that morning. Theresa was elated. Whoever she was, she'd gotten

under Malik's skin. Peyton Sawyer could be exactly
the cure Malik needed to fix what ailed him.

Peyton was excited as she stood in front of her first
class at NYU on Tuesday afternoon. She was teaching
"Introduction to Metropolitan Studies" and giving
students the basics on the urban environment. She'd
reviewed the list of agencies that supported the Metropolitan Studies intern program. There were many great
agencies in need, but when she'd received a call from
the assistant director at the Harlem Community Center,
the choice had been made for her.

Theresa had expressed a need for volunteers at the
center and Peyton jumped at the opportunity to have her
class participate. This was exactly the kind of practical experience students in her class needed—those who might
have an interest in social work or just in making a difference. And not only would she be asking her students to
volunteer, but Peyton herself intended to take part.

It was one of the things she wished she'd shared in
common with her husband, a desire to help others.
David had always moaned and groaned when she and
her mother Lydia volunteered or campaigned for a good
cause. He didn't mind writing a check, but physical
labor? Forget about it! Despite his shortcomings,
though, she'd loved him for years. Heck, they were
teenage sweethearts. She hadn't tried to change him;
she'd just loved and accepted him for who he was.
Maybe one day she'd find a man as dedicated as she to
community service.

"One of the best ways to learn about the community
and the social welfare system is to get involved," Peyton
said, beginning to end her lecture. "Which is why I want
all of you to volunteer at the Harlem Community Center.

There are many areas that might interest you, such as the computer center, day and afterschool care, sports or the arts. There is something for everyone."

As students signed up, one struck Peyton immediately. A beautiful young woman dressed rather plainly in what looked like secondhand clothes. "My name is Kendra Jackson. But I have to tell you, Professor Sawyer, I don't have a whole lot of time on my hands."

Caramel-colored, Kendra had big expressive eyes, but with some sadness. It made Peyton want to befriend her. "I understand, but volunteer work will give you practical experience to apply the principles you've learned in class. Is there anything I can do to help?"

"Well, you see, I have a six-month-old daughter," Kendra replied. "And my grandmother looks after her during the day, so I really have to get home."

"Why don't you bring her with you?" Peyton suggested. "The community center has a day care."

"They do?"

"Yes, they do," Peyton replied and widened the circle so the other students could hear. "And they need all of your help. They've lost their summer volunteers and would like us to start right away." Peyton rallied the troops. "Can you all come with me this afternoon? I believe there is some preliminary paperwork that you have to fill out before getting started, as well as having to attend a new-volunteer information session. And I'm sure if we discuss your situation, it shouldn't be a problem, Kendra."

"You mean you're coming too?" Kendra asked. "Why? You're the professor, you don't need extra credit." Several students chuckled.

"I'm coming because I want to help," Peyton returned. "I practice what I preach." Half a dozen faces smiled back at her. She'd won them over. "I'll see you all back here at four p.m. sharp and we'll head over to the center together."

"Why are you smiling like a cat that just ate a canary?" Malik inquired when Theresa poked her head in his office later that afternoon. Theresa was beaming like a neon light. It was clear she was proud of herself.

"Oh, I just found us a group of volunteers from NYU," Theresa answered. "They'll be stopping by any minute for a new-volunteer information session."

"Wow, you sure didn't waste any time," Malik said. He couldn't recall a time when Theresa had moved so quickly, which meant she had something up her sleeve. "What gives, Theresa?"

"Nothing," Theresa said, smiling. "We needed help and I got it."

"You sure did," Malik said. "You're a gem, Theresa."

"I know."

The phone rang and Theresa picked it up. "Great, thanks," Theresa hung up the receiver. "The volunteers are here."

"I'd like to meet them." Malik rose from his chair. "You know, introduce them to the center."

"I think that's an excellent idea."

"Aren't you coming?" Malik asked.

"No, uh, I have a lot of work to do." Theresa backed out of the door. "I'm sure you can handle it."

"All right." Malik eyed her suspiciously one final time before walking down the hall to the meeting room. He found over a dozen young men and women listening to the volunteer coordinator go over the application process, which included a photo and videotape release,

NY State central registry check and professional and personal release forms.

Malik was proud to see today's youth giving back to the community. It warmed his heart—until he saw the woman sitting in the front row holding center stage. *What is Peyton Sawyer doing here?*

When the volunteer coordinator, Denise Burke, looked up and saw Malik at the door, she waved him forward. "I'd like all of you to meet Malik Williams, the director of the Harlem Community Center."

When Peyton heard his name, her heart jolted. *No, say it isn't so. How could* he *be the director of the center?* Peyton wished she could snap her fingers and disappear. Instead, she sat with her attention towards Denise Burke. She saw him glance her way out of the corner of her eye as he walked towards the front, but she kept her eyes straight ahead.

"Thank you *all...*" Malik emphasized the word as he stood beside the coordinator "...for coming. It really means a lot." He touched his chest. "Just to give you a little history, the Harlem Community Center was founded in nineteen fifty-eight, and more than five hundred families and children use the center each and every day..."

Peyton couldn't hear a word Malik said, because she was fixed on the man himself. She studied him underneath hooded lashes and watched as he tossed back his dreads when he became exuberant. Even in faded blue jeans and a T-shirt, Malik had a swagger about him that caused Peyton to feel flushed. *Why was she having such a strong physical attraction to this man?* She couldn't understand it. She'd never thought of herself as someone unable to control herself, but Malik Williams was causing all sorts of heated sensations to flow through her body.

"The center is here to inspire the young people in this

community to use education and leadership to transcend difficult circumstances," Malik continued. "I am one of those people, ladies and gentleman. I, along with several of my close friends, grew up using this center, and today I'm privileged to work here and give back to all the community that contributed to my success. That being said, I welcome you to the Harlem center and hope you enjoy your volunteer experience. If there is anything that you need, please feel free to come and see me. My door is always open." Malik bowed and then headed for the door, but not before saying, "Professor Sawyer, a word if you please, outside."

Peyton thought about ignoring his request as if she hadn't heard him, but several curious sets of eyes were looking at her, so she had no choice.

"What are you doing here? And what kind of game are you playing?" Malik asked, once the doors had closed.

Peyton's brow furrowed. "What are you talking about?"

"I wasn't good enough for you to talk to, let alone spend time with, but now you come into *my* center acting like you're here to help people?" Malik's voice rose slightly.

"It's not an act," Peyton replied sternly. "I had no idea you were director when I picked this establishment. I wanted to volunteer as I'd done in Ohio, and give my students some practical experience. That's it, nothing more. You're just angry because I turned down your offer to show me around New York."

"And the only reason you turned me down was because you were attracted to me," Malik replied with a smile.

Was it that obvious? Peyton wondered. "I am not," she lied.

"I think you're scared." Malik came towards her until he was inches away from her face. He watched her take a step back. He was so close, he could smell the exotic scent of her perfume. "Scared of going after what you want, scared of dating someone different than your norm, scared of dating outside the box."

She didn't like that he'd hit the nail on the head, and yelled, "How dare you!" She realized just how loud she was, when several of her students turned and stared at her through the glass, so she lowered her voice. "You don't even know me."

"What I know is that I will not play a game of cat-and-mouse with you, so consider your services no longer needed." He turned on his heel and began walking away, even though he desperately wanted to pull the scared little professor into his arms and kiss her senseless.

He didn't get the opportunity because Theresa came storming towards him. "Malik Williams, what's going on here? I heard loud voices."

"You can't fire me. I'm volunteering!" Peyton stomped her foot.

Malik turned around. He hated that even her pouty face was so damn sexy. "*I* am the final word at this center, Ms. Sawyer," Malik yelled over his shoulder before sauntering past Theresa into his office and shutting the door behind him.

"He can't fire me, can he?" Peyton asked, turning to Theresa. "I mean, I'm here to help. I want to help and be here with my students."

"He is the director," Theresa said, shrugging, even though inside she was dying to laugh aloud. Everything had worked better than she'd hoped. Peyton had ruffled Malik's feathers again, which meant he found her more intriguing than the other women in his life. "But I can talk to him if you're serious." Theresa stared back at

Peyton. Did this woman have the fortitude to handle a man as strong and bullheaded as Malik?

"Of course, I'm serious. I believe in helping the community," Peyton replied. "I can give you several references at other centers, shelters and hospitals where I've volunteered."

Theresa smiled. "Once he calms down, I'll talk to him. Just fill out the paperwork, and by the time you come back I'll have it all worked out."

"Thank you." Peyton squeezed Theresa's hand. "You're a lifesaver." She went back inside to finish listening to the information session, while Theresa thought about how she would continue to stoke the flame.

"Malik, you're being unreasonable." Theresa barged into his office several minutes later. He was sitting with his mentor, Andrew Webster, the former director of the community center.

"Andrew, it's so good to see you, sweetheart." Theresa came forward and gave him a kiss on the cheek. "When did you arrive?"

"A few moments ago," Andrew returned. Even at sixty-five, Andrew looked as healthy as a horse. At six foot six, he towered over most men, including Malik, which is why he'd always managed to put the fear of God into him as a youth.

"Andrew just dropped by to discuss the upcoming 'Feed the Homeless' event before we were interrupted," Malik said, eyeing Theresa.

"Well, if you weren't acting like such a horse's behind," Theresa retorted, "I wouldn't have had to interrupt you."

"What's going on?" Andrew looked at his two former colleagues.

"There's a volunteer that is not suited for the center,"

Malik responded. He had no problem discussing the situation with his mentor. He valued Andrew's opinion. Because of him, he'd taken an interest in community service.

"Does he or she have a criminal background or health issues?" Andrew inquired.

"Well…not that I know of." Malik had no real cause to disapprove of Peyton Sawyer, other than that she was a tease.

"She's a great candidate," Theresa spoke up and closed the door behind her. "She's a professor at NYU and has encouraged many of her students to volunteer at the center. They're in orientation right now."

"So your beef is personal?" Andrew asked.

"She turned him down for a date," Theresa revealed.

Andrew turned to Malik. "So she damaged your ego. Is that it?"

"Before she knew who I was, she insulted me. Peyton Sawyer probably thought I was a lowly bohemian, and beneath her, a college-educated professor. I don't want that kind of person at the center. The people here need help. I won't have her making them feel inferior."

"Don't you think you might be overreacting a tad?" Andrew asked. He'd known Malik for years and this wouldn't be the first time he'd seen his protégé's quick temper. "You *do* recall your behavior a few months ago with Quentin, don't you? Why don't you go talk to the woman—you know? See what she's truly about before you leap to judgment. I think you could stand to learn a lesson from the past."

Trust Andrew to be so rational, so logical. Malik supposed that's why he looked up to him. Andrew had been the only father figure he had ever had. His biological father had skipped town shortly after he was born, leaving his mother to raise him on her own. That's until she hooked up with his stepfather Joe Johnson. *Did growing up in Joe's shadow give him his fiery temper?*

"Fine, I'll talk to her," Malik conceded, "but I make no guarantees."

"That's all I ask," Theresa said, and then winked at Andrew.

NYU was Malik and Sage's old stomping grounds. He loved the carnival-like atmosphere of Washington Square Park, with the dog-walkers, skateboarders, musicians and chess players. He'd called ahead to find out Peyton Sawyer's next class time and headed straight there. Class hadn't yet started, so Malik was able to blend in with the other one hundred or so students waiting to hear her lecture.

Malik was surprised when Peyton arrived in a short black skirt that revealed a generous amount of leg, and a sleeveless blue knit top that showed off her buff arms. Instead of prim and proper in tweeds and a button-down shirt, like most NYU professors. Malik was sure all the young men in the room were salivating just as he was.

Malik was mesmerized as he watched Peyton lecture for the next hour, and not just because of her sheer beauty, but more so because she showed a genuine passion for her work. He rarely saw that kind of enthusiasm. Her students' response and the discussion were a clear indication of how much she stimulated their minds. Malik was impressed.

"Your first paper will be due in two weeks. In a few days, my assistant will have the lecture notes online."

Malik waited until after most of her students had filed out before approaching Peyton.

Peyton was packing up her books when she felt a presence behind her. She whirled around and was shocked to find Malik Williams standing there. "What are you doing here?" The moment the words were out of her mouth, she realized how accusatory she sounded. Could it be because Malik looked like he could easily fit in with the Greenwich Village crowd, in cargo pants and a tight T-shirt? The shirt revealed his muscular arms and tight abs.

"Sounds familiar, huh?" Malik asked. His tone suggesting that he'd been as disconcerted as she when he'd found her on *his* turf.

Peyton ignored him and threw books into her satchel. "What do you want, Malik?"

Malik bowed his head. "I'm here to apologize. I was wrong about your intentions."

Peyton turned back around. "You're admitting you're wrong?"

"Yes, I am." Malik stood up straight. "I was wrong about your reasons for coming to the center, and after sitting in on your class and hearing how passionate you are about serving the community, I'm here to tell you that you can volunteer at the center."

Peyton chuckled. Should she be grateful that he'd had a change of heart? Perhaps. But he hadn't been completely off the mark, either, when he'd said she was scared of her attraction to him. She had never felt that kind of instant attraction. Not even with David; their relationship had been more of a slow burn. "I fully intended to do that. With or without your blessing, but I will accept your apology."

"Thank you," Malik said, smiling. "And if you let me, I'd like to make it up to you. How about a cup of coffee?"

"Are you asking me out *again?*" Peyton asked.

Malik took a deep breath. She really wanted to bust his chops. "I am asking you out for coffee."

Peyton debated with herself. Should she go? It was just coffee, after all. Perhaps if she went out with him and satisfied her curiosity once and for all, she could get back on an even keel. "All right." Peyton threw her satchel over her shoulder. "Lead the way."

Malik and Peyton took a short walk through Washington Square Park to Caffe Reggio. Always crowded, they managed to grab an outside table just as a couple was leaving. "Good looking out," Peyton commented.

"This was always a favorite hangout of mine when I went to NYU," Malik said as he helped her into her chair.

"Thank you." Peyton inhaled deeply and received a whiff of Malik's musky cologne. He smelled darn good.

A waitress appeared several moments later and took their order. Malik ordered a cappuccino and a cannoli and Peyton couldn't resist ordering their homemade tiramisu with her caffe latte.

"How did you get in the community service field?" Peyton asked, making polite chit-chat.

"Because I experienced firsthand how difficult it was for my mother, a single woman, to raise a child on her own. She didn't have the resources that are available today. If she did, maybe things would have turned out differently."

Peyton was curious about Malik's comment, she wondered if it had something to do with the fact that he and his friends frequented the center in their youth; but when he didn't expound further she didn't press for more details. The waitress came back and placed their coffees and Italian pastries on the table.

"Would you like anything else?"

"No, we're good for now," Malik replied, and the waitress departed.

"So, how long have you been director at the Harlem center?"

"For about five years, since my mentor retired."

"Sounds like he was a big influence."

"You've no idea," Malik replied, sipping his cappuccino. "Sometimes though, it feels like I'm fighting an uphill battle. We always need more equipment, more supplies, more food…" His voice trailed off.

"But you persevere," Peyton said.

"Yes." Malik nodded. He'd never stop fighting. "But we could use a corporate sponsor dedicated to our center. Anyway, enough about me." Malik turned the tables. "What made you decide to pack up your bags and move to New York? Usually, only starving artists hoping to catch their big break purposely move here."

"Not necessarily true," Peyton replied. "Sometimes people move because they need a change. When I put some feelers out and found that NYU had a position, I applied. Of course, it helped that my brother lived here."

She grew reflective. "My mother is a teacher too, and she's always been passionate about giving back. She used to take me with her to the homeless shelters, and if there was an event going on at my school, like a clothing or food drive, she was all over it."

"Sounds like she's a phenomenal woman."

"I respect her a lot. She's inspired me to volunteer, which is why I came to HCC." Then she added, "I had no idea you were the director."

"And if you *did* know you would have run in the opposite direction?" he wondered aloud. "What is it about me that disturbs you, Peyton?"

The way he said her name was like a soft caress, and it sent a little shiver up Peyton's spine. He was staring at her so intently, waiting for her response, that Peyton lost her words.

"Is it because you're married or otherwise engaged?" Malik asked the question he'd been dying to ask since they'd met. Peyton wasn't wearing a wedding ring, but that didn't mean anything these days.

"I'm single," she said softly.

"So there's no reason why we can't spend time together?"

"Isn't that what we're doing now?"

"Coffee during the day hardly counts," Malik countered. "How about we take it slow, and when you're ready we'll go out on a real date."

Peyton breathed a sigh of relief. "I think that could work."

"Now, can we just enjoy the ambience?" Malik asked.

Peyton smiled. "That sounds great."

They whiled away the rest of the afternoon sipping their coffee and talking politics, food, movies and music. They discovered a common love of democracy, sushi, sweets, dramas and jazz.

It was nearly evening when Malik walked Peyton to her office. She'd left several books that she needed for her next article. Peyton explained that the head of the Metropolitan Studies department expected the department's professors to have articles published in the education journals each year, so Peyton had to get cracking.

"Well, I have to admit I enjoyed the afternoon, Malik Williams." Peyton extended her hand when they made it to the building.

"So did I." Malik brushed his lips across Peyton's hand. She'd let her defenses down long enough for him to see a different side of her. "And I look forward to seeing you at the center." He gave her a broad smile before walking away.

Peyton started towards the entrance but couldn't resist looking back. When she did, Malik waved at her before crossing the street. He had definitely captured her interest. The question was, what was she going to do about it?

Chapter 3

When Quentin called him later during the week Malik said, "Hey, Q, what's up?"

"Two things, actually," Quentin began. "I spoke with a friend of mine at *Manhattan Weekly,* and he would like to do a feature on you for the newspaper. You know, showcase the center and hopefully drum up some support. And if that doesn't work—"

"Then what?" Malik asked. "What aren't you saying, Q?"

"Well…last week, you mentioned that you needed a corporate sponsor to contribute a donation solely to the Harlem center."

"Do you have someone in mind?"

"I do, and he'd like to meet with you over lunch on Monday, if you're interested?"

"Of course I'd be interested." Malik would jump at

the chance to discuss a corporate contribution for renovating the center and updating their technology.

"Great, I'll see you then."

When Malik hung up the phone, he realized Quentin hadn't told him who the meeting was with. Malik shrugged it off. Anyone who would contribute to the center was okay in his book.

"So, how's the background check coming on our volunteers?" Malik asked, walking into Theresa's office.

"Good. None of the students have any records."

"And Ms. Sawyer?" Malik inquired.

"What do you want to know?" Theresa asked, raising a brow.

"I don't know. Was there anything interesting?" Malik was curious about what was beneath that cool surface.

"Nope, not a thing," Theresa lied. There *was* something. On the central registry check, Peyton indicated a maiden name, which meant she was probably divorced, but Theresa wasn't going to tell Malik, because he'd just get in his own way. Better to let him find out on his own.

"Glad to hear it," Malik said. Peyton was a vibrant woman that he was not only attracted to but actually liked. She not only shared his passion for helping others, but championed it. He'd been waiting all his life for a woman that shared his convictions. Was it possible that he'd found her?

Peyton was working on her next lecture when she heard a knock on her office door. She looked up and found Kendra standing in her doorway. "Kendra! Hi." Peyton smiled and motioned her forward. "C'mon on in and have a seat."

"Thank you, Dr. Sawyer." Kendra sat down in the chair across from her and dropped her knapsack.

"What brings you by?" Peyton inquired. It wasn't unusual for students to stop in during her office hours for advice on what classes to take or just to talk about college life. But Peyton suspected there was more to Kendra's visit.

"Well…" Kendra lowered her head. "It doesn't look like I'm going to be able to volunteer."

"Why not?" Peyton asked. "The volunteer coordinator indicated it wouldn't be a problem for you to leave your daughter in day care."

"I know, but my boyfriend is very upset. He doesn't like the fact that I'm spending all this time in class; and if I volunteered, there wouldn't be any time for him."

Peyton took a deep breath. "I have to ask, Kendra, what is more important to you? Spending time with your boyfriend or getting a quality education?" Peyton took off her reading glasses. "Volunteering and understanding the needs of a community are vital if you want to go into this field."

"School, of course," Kendra answered, insulted. "I already had to take a semester off to have Tamara, and I'm back now. Omar takes care of us."

"Kendra, there are a lot of options and programs available to you as a single parent. You don't have to rely solely on your boyfriend."

"That's easy for you to say, Professor Sawyer. Not so easy when you have to feed an six-month-old."

"Perhaps I could talk to him on your behalf," Peyton offered. Although, she'd only been to a few lectures, Peyton saw promise in Kendra. During class, she was quick to speak up and offer her opinions and ideas.

"You would do that?" Kendra was surprised.

A knock sounded on Peyton's door before she could respond. Amber waved to her from the door. "Excuse me,

Kendra," Peyton apologized and glanced up. "Amber, give me a few minutes okay?"

"Sure." Amber eyed her suspiciously before walking away.

"Of course I would help," Peyton said, finally answering Kendra's question. "I want you to succeed. So, if you'd like bring him by. We can all talk and maybe come up with a solution that would work for everyone. How does that sound?"

"I guess it's worth a try," Kendra said, picking her knapsack off the floor. "But I warn you, Professor Sawyer, Omar can be somewhat of a jerk."

"He wouldn't be the first I've encountered," Peyton replied, rising from her chair. She walked Kendra to the door and poked her head out looking for Amber. She found her leaning up against the wall.

"You ready?" Amber asked.

"Give me a sec to get my purse." Peyton rushed inside her office and pulled her purse out of the desk drawer and slung it over her shoulder. "I'm ready," she said seconds later.

They left the building and went over to the faculty dining hall. Amber waited until they'd ordered summer salads before homing in on Peyton.

"Peyton, Peyton, Peyton," Amber shook her head. "You have to learn not to get so involved in your students' affairs."

Peyton's mouth curled into a grimace. "What do you mean? I was only trying to help."

"It's just not a good idea," Amber replied, "to get so *personally* involved."

"If I can help a student, then I'm going to do it," Peyton stated firmly. As a teacher, she'd seen her mother help many students, and Peyton strived to do the same. "How difficult can it be, anyway?"

For his meeting with Quentin and the corporate sponsor, Malik dressed extra-carefully. He wanted to impress the bigwig, if he was going to convince him to hand over thousands of dollars. He chose a black, double-breasted suit and teamed it with a starched white shirt. He nixed a tie, because he hated the darn things, and he left a few buttons open at the top. Dark loafers, which he'd bought from a local street vendor, completed his ensemble. Malik admired himself in the mirror. He rarely, if ever, got dressed to come to the center, unless he had a meeting at the CAN headquarters, or the board was making their semi-annual visit.

Malik finished up paperwork in the morning before meeting Quentin at The Grill Room. "I have a twelve o'clock with Quentin Davis," Malik informed the maître d', once he arrived.

"Follow me." He led Malik across the marble-floored dining room to a table with a view overlooking the Hudson River, where Quentin and Avery were already seated. *What is* she *doing here?* Malik wondered.

"Avery, Quentin," Malik nodded as he came towards the table.

"It's good to see you, Malik," Avery said, smiling.

Malik sat down and the maître d' placed a napkin over his lap. "Enjoy your lunch," the maître d' said.

"Thank you. I'm surprised to see you here, Avery, but happy that you could join us," Malik responded and turned to his best friend. "Q, I have to thank you for this opportunity, because the center could use a makeover."

"Don't thank me yet," Quentin looked towards the doorway.

"Why would you say that?" Malik asked, then his eyes followed Quentin's, to see corporate tycoon Richard King walking towards them. Malik blinked several times to make sure his eyes weren't deceiving him, but when he opened them Richard King was standing right in front of him.

"Malik." Richard extended his hand—which Malik declined.

Malik inwardly seethed. Just a few months ago Richard King had wanted to tear down the community center and build a multimedia complex and condos, but Malik and CAN had fought him hard. What in the world would possess Q to think that he would ever accept a donation from the man who tried to destroy the very thing he was working so hard to preserve?

What Malik wanted to do was tell King that he could take his money and shove it, but he heard Andrew's voice telling him not to be so quick to judge. He busied himself by reaching for the pitcher of water and pouring himself a glass.

"Richard." Avery rose and kissed her biological father's cheek. Not many people knew that she was the product of an interracial relationship. Richard had once had an affair with Avery's mother, an African-American woman. Even though they hadn't acknowledged each other publicly, only finding out they were related earlier this spring, she and Richard had begun to form a tentative friendship.

"How are you?" She attempted to make conversation, even though Malik was shooting daggers at both her and Quentin.

Avery had already gone out on a limb a few months ago when she'd asked Richard not to go forward with his Harlem development plans. When she'd approached him with the idea of doing a flip and renovating the center, to show his commitment to the community, initially he'd been hesitant. But she'd persuaded him to at least come and listen; but now Malik's attitude threatened to ruin all her hard work.

"Well, darling," Richard said, and smiled. It warmed his heart to have a relationship with the only biological child he'd ever have since his wife, Cindy, and he had been unable to conceive. "Quentin." He leaned over and shook the photographer's hand.

After the waiter came and took their drink and lunch orders, Quentin dispensed with the pleasantries and got right down to business. "We all know why we're here." He glanced at Malik, who was conspicuously quiet and sat sipping his water. "Harlem Community Center is in need of renovation. The center is looking for a corporate sponsor. Malik, why don't you explain to Richard some of the community center's needs?"

Malik inhaled deeply and willed down the bile that was in his throat, then took on a professional air. "HCC needs a corporate sponsor dedicated to our center and willing to put up the funds for remodeling. We need new paint, carpeting and tile throughout, plus refinishing the gymnasium floor and updating the kitchen. The computer facility is in desperate need of new technology. The game room could use another foosball machine and a new ping-pong table. We'd also like to set up some type of reserve for any special projects that we'd like to complete in the future."

"You don't need a lot." Richard chuckled.

"Are you laughing at the needs of the common folk?" Malik asked.

"Of course he wasn't," Avery said, defending him, "but that was quite a laundry list. Isn't that right?" Avery's green eyes landed on Quentin's for help.

"Yes, but trust me, Richard, when we—" Quentin glanced at Malik, wanting his friend to know that they were all in this together "—say that it's all needed."

"I don't doubt that it is."

"But you're wondering what's in it for you?" Malik asked, as the tycoon sat back and stared at him. "I would say the satisfaction of knowing that you're helping a great many people, but since I doubt that's the answer you're looking for, then I would say the positive press that it would generate, given your portrayal in the media as a ruthless tycoon. And of course, the tax relief."

"Malik, that's enough!" Avery said. She was embarrassed by his rudeness.

"Let the man speak his mind, Avery. He's entitled to his opinion," Richard replied, "no matter how wrong it might be. If I were as ruthless as you say, Mr. Williams, I would have gone through with the development deal despite my daughter's plea. And I most certainly wouldn't be here listening to you today."

"Touché. But then it begs the question, why are you here?" Malik pressed. "Are you here to assuage your conscience?"

"I'm here because your center needs funding and I can provide it, but if you'd rather look elsewhere…" Richard left his words hanging in the air.

"What I would like is to be able to look myself in the mirror and be proud of the man looking back at me." Malik rose from his chair and threw his napkin down. "I'm not at all sure I can do that, knowing that the King Corporation would be the sponsor. Quentin and Avery." Malik turned to his friend. "Thanks for trying, but I don't think this is the right fit for the center. Richard, good day." Malik turned on his heel and strode out of the restaurant.

"Malik, wait!" Quentin yelled, but he was already gone.

* * *

Malik fumed on the train ride back to Harlem. Of all the potential corporate sponsors in Manhattan, Richard King was definitely not the person he'd expected to see when Quentin asked him to lunch. His cell phone had rung several times since he'd left the restaurant, and he let all the calls go to voice mail. He was in no mood to talk to Q right now.

Malik knew who was behind the ambush: Avery. Quentin would have never thought about approaching the man who tried to tear down the center to ask for money. Malik was beginning to think his boy was whipped.

As he exited the train and walked back to the center, Malik removed his overcoat. Even though he looked good in them, he dreaded monkey suits. "Loretta," he smiled at the receptionist when he came inside.

"Malik." She smiled back at him. She couldn't resist thinking what a fine-looking young man he was. *My granddaughter could sure use a fellow like him, instead of that good-for-nothing she hung out with.*

"Is Theresa in her office?"

"Yes, sir."

Malik didn't bother knocking, and just stormed in. "You will not believe who the corporate mogul was that Q wanted me to meet."

"Well excuse you," Theresa huffed, placing her hand over the mouthpiece. "I am on the phone."

"I'm sorry, Theresa," Malik replied sheepishly, looking down. He mouthed the words "Come talk to me" and left the room.

Several minutes later, Theresa found Malik reclining in his chair and staring at the ceiling. "I take it the meeting did not go as you anticipated."

"Worse," Malik responded, sitting up. "Quentin and Avery had the nerve to set up a meeting with Richard King, of all people."

Understanding dawned on Theresa. "Ah! And there's the rub."

"What was he thinking?" Malik said. "Richard King! I swear, Quentin is led around by the nose."

"The man is in love," Theresa said.

"Yeah, well, love has fried his brain."

"Please don't be upset with him." Theresa pleaded Quentin's case. "I know he was only trying to help."

"I'm not angry at him." Malik tossed his head. "Being angry takes too much energy. We're just back to the drawing board."

"Don't worry, Malik." Theresa came forward and patted his shoulder. "Trust me, okay. This isn't the first time the center's been in need. Over the years, I've seen Andrew down and out like this, but believe you me, if there's a will, there's a way. I have faith in you."

Malik gave a halfhearted smile. *Why couldn't he have had a mother like Theresa Harris?*

"Is Malik here?" Peyton asked the receptionist later that afternoon in the community center lobby. She'd decided, spur-of-the-moment, after her last class let out at four to come by the center and ask for Malik's assistance with Kendra's situation. She was hoping he could share some insight or know of some programs that might help the young mother. She glanced at her watch, it was well past five, but she was hoping that Malik was as much of a workaholic as she.

"Let me check with his assistant," Loretta replied. "Please have a seat."

Peyton was about to sit down when the door flew open. "Hi, Peyton. What can I do for you?"

"Well…" Peyton was hoping to speak with Malik directly. Much to her own surprise, she hadn't been able to stop thinking about him. He radiated a vitality that drew her like a magnet. And now she was here at the center, hoping the sexy director with deliciously long dreads would join her for dinner to discuss Kendra's situation.

"Peyton?" Theresa noticed that the professor had a dreamy expression on her face. "You were saying?"

Peyton shook her head. "I was hoping Malik might give me some more information about day care and assistance for young mothers. Is he in?"

Theresa smiled knowingly. The professor had come in person to get information she could have researched on the Internet or gotten via the phone. Peyton Sawyer was definitely interested in Malik, and Theresa was going to stoke the flame. "Sure. Let me get him for you. He's just finishing up a phone call."

Malik was completely caught off guard when Theresa told him that Peyton Sawyer was in the lobby waiting for him. He quickly checked his appearance in the mirror before coming out.

She stood when he arrived, allowing him to lazily appraise her toned athletic legs extending from her straight black skirt, which she'd accompanied with a black-and-white polka dot, silk shirt and a single strand of pearls. She looked like the cherry on top of a sundae and he wanted to gobble her up. "Peyton, it's good to see you."

There was a tingle in the pit of her stomach as he said her name. "You too," Peyton managed to say. His nearness was making her senses spin.

"What can I do for you?" he asked.

Having Malik stare at her intensely with those dark brown eyes caused Peyton to get tongue-tied. "Well, I…I came to see if I couldn't tempt you with some sushi. As I recall, you know a great place."

"Are you asking me out on a date?" Malik queried.

"It's not really a date," Peyton lied. "I need your professional advice, and I just thought it might be easier to discuss over dinner."

"Oh really?"

Malik grinned, and when he did Peyton could see he had dimples. *Why hadn't she noticed that before?* "Yes, really."

"If you say so," Malik replied. She'd come all this way *for him.* "But in answer to your question, yes, I would love to go out for sushi. Just let me get my jacket."

"All right." Peyton turned away as he left and tried to collect herself. Her heart was thumping so loudly in her chest; Peyton swore the receptionist could hear it.

Malik returned with his suit jacket over his arm. "Ready?"

"Yes." Peyton didn't mind it one bit when Malik placed his hand on the small of her back and guided her out the door. She liked a man who took charge.

Malik hailed a cab with ease, and soon they were seated and on their way to Hatsuhana on Forty-eighth Street. When the host wanted to seat them at a table Peyton balked. "Can we sit at the bar?" She'd noticed two open seats in front of the chefs. "I love to watch the chef's showmanship."

"Absolutely." The host sat them at the bar.

Malik pulled out a bar stool and slid it underneath her before sitting next to her.

"Doesn't the fresh fish look great?" The displays housed fresh tuna, salmon, yellowtail, whitefish, shrimp and a lot else Peyton didn't recognize, but she made polite conversation to avoid the elephant in the room.

"I'm flattered by your dinner offer." Malik perused the menu, even though he already knew what he wanted. He always ordered the tuna and California rolls.

"I admit we got off to a shaky start, but this dinner really was about helping a student," she said, glancing sideways at him.

"You don't need an excuse to ask me out." Malik turned and faced her. "I like you, Peyton. And I'd like to know you even better. Don't you want the same?"

"I am not afraid of you, Malik, if that's what you're implying," Peyton replied. "I'm just treading lightly."

"Ah, there's more you're not saying," Malik deduced, rubbing his jaw. When she tried to speak, he placed an index finger on her lips. "And you don't have to tell me. There's no pressure here, Peyton. When you're ready I'll listen." Whatever she was holding back was big. Malik just hoped that in time she would feel like she could trust him. "So, what are you having?" he asked, changing the subject.

Her lips tingled from his touch. "Thank you." Peyton smiled. "And I think I'll have the tempura-battered fish and veggies." After they'd placed their order, Peyton brought up Kendra's situation. "My student is monetarily dependent upon her boyfriend, who resents that she's in school. Since I'm new to the area, I was hoping you might know of some assistance programs?"

"First off, she should start with the New York Department of Family Assistance and their OTDA department," Malik said with authority.

"What does that stand for?"

"The Office of Temporary and Disability Assistance," Malik informed her. "She can apply for food stamps and even go after child support if she wants."

"What about financial assistance?" Peyton inquired.

"They can provide that too, under their temporary assistance program, for up to sixty months. So there's a lot of help out there, if she's willing to go after it."

"Thank you so much, Malik." Peyton patted his knee. "I'll be sure and pass the info on to my student."

"You're welcome." Malik placed his large hand over hers. When she didn't quickly move it away, Malik knew they'd crossed a bridge and he had a real shot at getting better acquainted. He liked that she was so caring and sympathetic to those less fortunate. It was rare that he found someone that shared his passion for helping others. He supposed that's why he was so attracted to Peyton because she was beautiful on the inside and out.

"What about you? How was your day?" Peyton asked. "It must be something big, with the suit and all. I didn't think that was really your style, though you do wear it well." The suit fit his well-muscled body to perfection.

So she'd noticed, had she? Malik grinned. "Thank you, and you would be right in your assumption. I had a lunch appointment, but it didn't go as I envisioned."

"Why? What happened?" Peyton realized she sounded nosy, then added, "If you don't mind my asking."

"I'm looking for a corporate sponsor for the center."

"Is it in trouble?"

"No, but it could use some repair and renovation. Unfortunately, Children's Aid Network has to spread the funds around to so many centers that we don't always get what we need, when we need it. And today, I thought that would change. My friend Quentin, who you met the other night, set up a meeting with a potential corporate sponsor."

"And?"

"It turned out to be the very same man who a few short months ago wanted to tear us down to build multimillion-dollar condos and a mediaplex." Malik released a deep breath.

Peyton stared as if waiting for a better explanation. "I'm sorry. And the problem is—?"

"He's the man that tried to destroy this community."

"But if he's had a change of heart—" Peyton bunched her shoulders "—I don't see why not. So what if he sponsors the renovation to clear his guilty conscience? Either way, it's a win-win for him, as well as for the center. Don't you need the funds?"

"We do, but at what cost?" Malik asked. He had too much pride to accept a dime from Richard King.

"I guess only you can answer that," Peyton replied. "But if you want my advice, such as it is, I say go for it. And if you need help, I'll be there in whatever capacity you need."

Malik considered her words. He may have to rethink his position. Plus, Peyton was volunteering, even though she had no idea what that might entail. "Thanks, Peyton, I appreciate it. Now, can we stop talking shop?"

"That sounds like a good idea." Their conversation turned to other topics, and when their food arrived they washed the succulent vegetables and fresh fish down with plum wine, leaving Peyton feeling languid and more relaxed than she'd felt in years. Whenever she was around Malik, he had that effect on her. He made her want to forget the past and embrace the present.

When she finally glanced at her watch, Peyton realized the hour. She had a 10 a.m. class that she needed to prepare for, but she didn't want the night to be over. "As much as I'd love to stay…" Peyton began.

"It's time we left," Malik finished.

"Afraid so."

Malik quickly settled the bill, much to Peyton's chagrin. She'd asked him out and was prepared to pay for the meal, but he'd refused.

"Thanks for the dinner," Peyton said when the cab dropped her off in front of her Brooklyn brownstone a short while later.

"You're welcome," Malik said, hopping out. "Keep the meter running," he told the cab driver, and followed her up the steps to her door.

Peyton wasn't sure what to do. This was one of those awkward moments at the end of a date, so she said, "I had a lovely evening," and leaned in for a hug and a quick peck, but Malik turned his head so that her kiss landed on his lips instead of cheek.

Peyton was stunned at first, she hadn't expected that, but she didn't protest, either. The caress of his lips on her mouth set her aflame with desire. And when Malik took it a step further and deepened the kiss, invading her mouth with his tongue, Peyton moaned.

As the kiss became more passionate, Malik folded Peyton in his arms and pulled her firmly to him. He loved the taste of her and the feel of her breasts against his chest. His pulse raced as his hands dipped and settled firmly on her hips. Malik felt the hardness in his pants press up against Peyton. Carried away by his own response, he didn't even notice Peyton resisting—until she had pushed him away.

"I'm sorry. I can't..." Peyton's voice caught in her throat as mixed feelings surged through her. "I can't do this." Peyton opened her front door as fast as she could and bolted inside.

Malik was puzzled by the change in mood. What had he done wrong? Had he misread her response? He didn't think so. She'd kissed him back. He liked Peyton more

than any other woman he could remember, and hoped
he hadn't ruined one of the best things to come his way
in a long time.

Chapter 4

Peyton stood in front of her window on Wednesday morning and wondered what had gotten into to her. Why had she asked Malik to dinner? And how could she have let him kiss her? Peyton didn't know what upset her more, the fact that she should feel guilty and didn't, or that she'd enjoyed Malik's kisses. Here it was days after their passionate encounter, and she could still feel his lips on hers. Peyton rubbed her arms to stop goose bumps from forming.

When Amber stopped by her office with Starbucks cups in hand, Peyton motioned her in. She was dying to confide in her.

"You look deep in thought. Is something wrong?" Amber inquired, handing her a caffe latte.

"Thank you." Peyton accepted the drink. "And in answer to your question, plenty." Peyton walked back around to her chair.

"Well, fill me in." Amber sat down.

"I innocently asked Malik out the other night for dinner." Peyton took a sip of her coffee.

"Your honor, notice the word 'innocent,'" Amber said, acting as if Peyton were on the witness stand.

Peyton rolled her eyes and continued. "I asked him out to discuss Kendra's situation."

"And?"

"We had a lovely evening," Peyton responded. "He gave me some advice on programs for single mothers and then, like a gentleman, he escorted me home and walked me to my door. And then he kissed me."

"How was it?" Amber asked excitedly, placing her Starbucks cup on Peyton's maple desk and leaning forward.

Peyton opened her desk drawer and handed Amber a coaster. "It was wonderful and sweet and passionate, but then I bolted."

"Why in heavens would you do that?" Amber asked. "From the dreamy expression on your face when you described his kiss, you must have enjoyed it."

"Because things were moving too fast," Peyton replied. "You just don't understand, Amber."

"Yes I do," Amber replied. "And the first thing I know is that you need to stop thinking with your head and start feeling with your heart. Malik's a sexy guy, and he's made it clear from day one that he liked you. And it's obvious you like him, so why deny yourself? Run with it."

"It's not that simple," Peyton responded and turned towards the window.

"Explain it to me."

Peyton doubted Amber would understand. For as long as she'd known her, she'd always had a different man on her arm.

"I'm waiting…."

Peyton paused before finally speaking. "I'm *afraid,* okay?" She wiped a tear way with the back of her hand.

"Oh, Peyton." Amber jumped up and gave Peyton a hug. She was surprised that her friend, a tough-as-nails professor, feared anything. "What are you afraid of?"

"I haven't felt such a strong connection with any man since David died," she confessed. "My attraction to Malik scares me. You see, I have only been with one man."

"You mean sexually?" Amber asked.

"Of course I mean sexually," Peyton responded, pulling away. "David was my first and *only* lover." Peyton felt completely insecure in the sex department. She was a novice compared to most women these days. It's not like she and David hadn't experimented. He'd just been traditional when it came to their lovemaking. He'd always been the first to initiate sex and she'd followed his lead.

"Well, now I understand, but you shouldn't sweat it. It's like riding a bike. It all comes back to you."

Peyton smiled. "Easier said than done."

Amber touched Peyton's cheek. "Don't doubt yourself. You are a strong and sexy woman, Peyton. What you've endured would have broken many a person. I was one of the naysayers who thought you'd never get over David's death, but look at you, you're stronger than ever. Don't let fear hold you back, honey. Otherwise you might miss out on something really special."

As Peyton finished her afternoon lectures, Amber's words stayed with her. Peyton just wondered if she had the courage to move forward.

Malik sighed as the members of the Children's Aid Network Community Advisory Board dispersed from the conference room the following afternoon. He'd been unsuccessful in convincing them to give the Harlem center additional funds. The only good thing was that a reporter for *Manhattan Weekly* had come that morning and interviewed him. The story would run in next week's paper.

"How did it go?" Theresa asked enthusiastically, as she swung open the conference door.

"Don't ask," Malik said, slamming the folder shut.

Maybe next year or the next, they'd said. But the center couldn't wait that long. If he had the money, he could have the place painted and the floors done in a matter of weeks. Of course, the kitchen renovation would take a little longer. And then there was the computer center. With technology constantly changing, their equipment was outdated.

"They turned you down again?" Theresa asked.

"Afraid so. But then again, it wouldn't be the first time," Malik replied.

Several days ago, he'd sent a beautiful woman scurrying away, and he hadn't seen or heard a word from her in days. Her application had been approved and her background check came back clean, so there was no reason Peyton couldn't start volunteering immediately. Yet, the lovely professor still hadn't shown her face, and he had no one to blame but himself.

"Did something else happen?" Theresa was curious about Malik's comment.

"Nothing that I care to expound upon," Malik replied.

Theresa thought about pressing him for more information, but she could see that he was in one of his brooding moods. She remembered he used to have them as a youngster and she'd wondered what caused them. But he'd never talked about it. Malik had a tendency to be a loner at times. "All right, if you want to talk I'm here."

"Thanks, Theresa."

After he finished hiring a new doctor for the clinic staff, Malik closed up shop at the center and headed over to Dante's. He was meeting the guys for drinks and some much-needed advice. No offense to Sage, but he'd hadn't asked her to come along. He did have his pride, after all. And this was man's business.

"Malik." Dante smiled when he came in, but then, when he saw the sour expression on his friend's face, he changed course. "Don't tell me, 'cause I already know. A woman's got you down?"

"How'd you know?" Malik asked.

"What's the cause of most of our troubles?"

"Women!"

"Enough said," Dante replied, then went behind the bar and popped open a bottle of beer. He slid it across the countertop towards Malik.

"Thanks, man."

Quentin came in several minutes later and joined them. "Hey, Malik." Quentin sat down next to his stubborn friend. He hadn't heard from him since he'd invited Malik to lunch to meet Richard. Quentin could only assume that Malik was upset with him and had been giving him the silent treatment as he'd done a couple of months ago.

"Q," Malik said, nodding. "What's up?"

"You tell me," Quentin responded, rubbing his goatee. "A brother hasn't heard from you in days."

Malik shrugged. "Now c'mon, Q. You had to know that I wouldn't accept a penny from Richard King." Malik tipped back his bottle of beer and took a generous swig.

"So this was your way of punishing me?" Quentin sighed. Malik's temper was getting old. "I thought we'd gotten past this childishness, Malik."

"And we have," Malik replied, turning to Quentin. "The world does not revolve around you, Q. I do have other things on my mind."

An O formed on Quentin's lips. He hadn't thought about that.

"This brother is down and out about that professor at NYU," Dante offered.

"Oh, yeah." Quentin remembered the leggy mahogany babe that had caught Malik's eye. "She was pretty hot. So what happened?"

"I screwed it up," Malik replied and swigged his beer. "Came on too strong."

"But you can correct that," Quentin responded. "You know, tone down your enthusiasm."

"You didn't see her run in the opposite direction." Malik dragged his long, narrow fingers through his dreads.

"It's not too late," Dante said. "Isn't she going to be volunteering at the center?"

Malik nodded.

"Well then, show her that you can take things as slow as she wants," Dante continued, "Show her all that Malik Williams charm that we know you have."

"I guess."

"Not you guess, you know," Quentin stated. "The next time Peyton Sawyer sees you, be the perfect gentleman."

"Dr. Sawyer, may we come in?" Kendra asked from the doorway before class on Friday.

Peyton glanced up and saw Kendra standing with an imposing young man who she could only assume was Omar, Kendra's boyfriend and the father of her child. He was dressed in jeans and a sports jersey and wearing a baseball cap. Peyton surmised he was over six feet, and with his football player physique he could intimidate anyone—but not her. She'd failed several young men just like him when she'd been in Cleveland, those who'd thought their athletic scholarship guaranteed them a free ride. That's until they'd come to her class and discovered they actually had to work to earn a grade.

From the scowl on his face, it was clear Omar did not want to be here, but Peyton welcomed him anyway.

"Come on in," Peyton stood and extended her hand. "Please have a seat."

"Omar Bishop, this is Dr. Peyton Sawyer, my professor." Kendra smiled as they both sat across from Peyton.

Omar gave Peyton a cold stare. "And here I thought she was white." Omar laughed to himself.

"Mr. Bishop, there *are* black professors," Peyton responded. "And because I am a minority, I understand how important it is to get a quality education, which is what I want for Kendra."

"That's what *you* want, Doctor," Omar replied. "If it were up to me, Kendra here—" he roughly pulled Kendra toward him "—wouldn't work at all. She'd be content being my baby's mama. But now she's got all these ideas in her head about getting into social work."

"They are not ideas, Omar." Kendra pushed him away. She was extremely annoyed at his comment. "It's a career."

"One that would be well served by Kendra volunteering at the community center," Peyton said. "I took the liberty of pulling together some literature on the center as well as the areas she'd be exposed to when volunteering." Peyton leaned over to hand Omar several pamphlets.

When he didn't accept them, Kendra took them. "Thank you."

Omar clapped his hands slowly at Peyton's impassioned speech. "That's all well and good, *Dr. Sawyer,* but what's in this for you?" he asked, lounging back in the chair and staring back at her.

"What do you mean?"

"I said what do you get out of all this? Why are you helping Kendra? Because no one does something for nothing," Omar stated.

"I'm helping her because I believe in her talent," Peyton countered. "Don't you?"

"What I believe is that Kendra hardly has time for me *now,* and volunteering at some center won't help it none." Omar rose from his chair.

"But it might help." Peyton stood. She refused to believe that she could not get through to the young man.

"C'mon, baby." Omar grabbed Kendra by the hand and pulled her towards the door.

"I'm sorry." Kendra mouthed the words as she left.

Peyton threw the pen in her hand across the room, frustrated that now one of her most promising students was going to miss out on a great opportunity.

"Guess who's here?" Theresa poked her head inside Malik's office.

Malik shrugged. "I don't know, who?"

"Peyton Sawyer and her students. Denise arranged for them to help out in the day care and Headstart programs, as well as tutoring and homework assistance in our afterschool programs."

"Sounds great," Malik replied. "And what did Dr. Sawyer choose?"

"Mentoring," Theresa replied. "She wants to encourage African-American and Latina women and help out with the college preparatory program."

"Sounds right up her alley."

"Sure does. You should stop by and say hello," Theresa urged.

"Now really isn't a good time," Malik replied.

Theresa didn't understand. "All right." Malik had been so excited when Peyton had asked him to dinner last week, Theresa was sure they were headed in the right direction. What could have gone wrong?

Malik rose to his feet, grabbed his folder and rushed out the room before Theresa could say another word.

Once he found out her schedule, Malik continued avoiding Peyton for the rest of the week. He was walking back to his office on Friday afternoon after checking in with the center's business manager, Greg Burns, on the particulars for the homeless dinner that evening when he ran smack dab into the object of his desire in the hallway.

"Peyton," Malik gasped as she grabbed ahold of him to steady herself.

When she glanced up, he captured her eyes with his and Peyton's heart jolted and her pulse pounded. "Malik." She nodded when he released her. Peyton had wondered when she would run into the elusive director. "How are you?" She felt foolish for running off last week like a scared school girl.

"Good. And you?"

"Fine." Peyton watched Malik with a keenly observant eye, but she could read nothing from his expression. "I saw the article in *Manhattan Weekly,* congratulations."

"Thanks." Malik smiled. "I'm hoping it will help draw some sponsors."

"I'm sure it will," Peyton said, smiling.

"Okay, well I guess I'll see you later." Malik tried to make a fast getaway, but Peyton placed her hand on his forearm.

She felt the impulse to explain that she'd suffered a terrible tragedy and had been scared of forging ahead. Maybe, just maybe, she could try with him. "Malik, can we talk?" Peyton asked. She didn't realize she was still holding his arm until he glanced down. So she let go.

"Um, now isn't a good time, Peyton."

"You can't spare five minutes for a friend?"

"Is that what we are?" Malik looked deep into her eyes. The feelings she evoked in him and the kiss they'd shared had been far from friendly.

Peyton was about to respond when Theresa came bounding down the hall. "There you are!" Theresa exclaimed, out of breath.

"Were you looking for me?" Malik asked.

Theresa glanced at the couple. She could cut the tension between them with a knife. "No, for Peyton," she responded. "We're shorthanded for servers tonight for our dinner for the homeless and I was hoping she'd be willing to help out. That's if you don't have any plans for the evening?" Theresa looked hopefully up at Peyton, who was several inches taller than she.

"Sure." Peyton smiled. "I don't have any plans." She glanced in Malik's direction, but his face was stone. *Was he happy or upset that she would be staying?*

"Great, you're a lifesaver," Theresa said. "Carry on." She waved and nearly skipped away. She had stepped in just in the nick of time.

"Well, I have to go," Malik replied, walking backward. "Tons to do to make sure tonight goes off without a hitch."

Peyton sighed as she watched him walk away. She wanted to explain to Malik why she'd run, but he wasn't giving her the chance. She was going to have to create an opportunity.

* * *

As Peyton served spaghetti and meatballs to the homeless, her mind wandered to Kendra as she looked at her volunteer students. She had hoped that Kendra would have the fortitude to volunteer despite her boyfriend's lack of support, but she'd been wrong. Kendra was a no-show.

She was heading back to the kitchen to refill the empty foil pan with more spaghetti, when she caught Malik staring, but then he immediately looked away. Peyton wondered if she'd imagined the whole thing. As she filled the pan, Peyton vowed to tell Malik about her past, whether he liked it or not.

Malik sighed. Peyton had caught him staring. He couldn't resist watching her. She'd piled her shoulder-length hair on top of her head and out of her face, and didn't seem to mind that she was wearing her fashionable clothes underneath a stained apron. She'd pitched in on a moment's notice and hadn't hesitated to make marinara sauce or cut up onions.

Malik supposed that's what he liked about her, her willingness to give. He'd wanted to reach out to her tonight, but he didn't want to get rejected again.

On the other side of the room, Theresa caught Peyton glancing in Malik's direction as she placed garlic bread on several patrons' plates. "You know, all you have to do is talk to him." She bumped Peyton with her hip. "He doesn't bite."

Peyton laughed. "Are you sure about that?"

"Positive. Go ahead." Theresa pushed Peyton away. "I've got this covered."

"Thanks," Peyton replied. She caught Malik as he came back inside after throwing out the garbage. "Hey."

"Hey yourself. Great job on the spaghetti sauce." He'd seen several men wiping their plates with their garlic bread. "You're a hit with the locals."

"Thanks, but I didn't do too much, except doctor up the bottled stuff," Peyton admitted. "Listen, can you help in the pantry for a minute? There's a can I can't reach."

"Sure." Malik followed behind her and flicked on the light in the closet. "Which one?"

She pointed quickly to an unknown can. "The one on the top." Just as she fibbed, they both heard the door shut behind them. "What was that?" Peyton asked.

Malik walked over and turned the handle. They were locked in.

On the opposite side, Theresa smiled at her handiwork. Malik and Peyton needed some help in the communication department. Some time alone in a confined space might do the trick.

"Did you do this on purpose?" Malik asked, whirling around.

"Why in Heaven's name would I do that?" Peyton argued.

Malik reached up and pulled down a can of salmon. "Did you really need a can of pink salmon?"

Peyton couldn't resist bursting into laughter. "No, I suppose not, but you've been avoiding me all night. Make that all week. I had to resort to devious measures."

"After you ran off the other night, I thought that's what you wanted," Malik replied, eyeing her suspiciously.

"No, it's not." Peyton came forward and took Malik's large hand in her small one. "You were right. I was scared of what's happening between us."

"Why? I thought we'd connected."

"We did." Peyton lowered her head. "But there's a lot you don't know about me, Malik."

"Such as?"

"I was married."

Malik used his index finger and tilted her chin upward to look at him. "I hope by the word 'was' you mean past tense?"

"Yes, I do. You see," Peyton paused for several moments before she spoke softly, "my husband David died in a car crash five years ago. And I've only casually dated since."

"I see." Malik turned away. Now it all made sense. At least now Malik knew what he was up and against and could bow out gracefully. He wouldn't compete with a ghost.

"No, you don't." Peyton grabbed him by the arm. When he turned around, Peyton didn't like the look she saw in his eyes.

"I don't want or need your pity, Malik Williams. The reason I ran when you kissed me the other night is not because of David. It was because I'd never wanted another man as much as I wanted you that night."

Malik was stunned by her bold declaration. She and David had been so young they'd never really known anyone else but each other. But with Malik, she felt the passion of a woman fully aware of a man.

"You mean that?" he asked.

"Yes, I do."

Before Peyton could think, Malik crossed the short distance between them and pulled her into his arms. He captured her lips in an onslaught that sent fiery flames shooting through her. Malik was a seasoned kisser and did deliciously erotic things to her mouth, so that Peyton felt compelled to wrap her arms around his neck to keep from falling.

When his tongue entered her mouth, desire rushed

through Malik, and he brought Peyton's body closer to his. She tasted so good and so sweet, Malik wanted to ravish her in the pantry, but the door swung open moments later to reveal Theresa beaming from the doorway. "See, I knew all the two of you needed was a little one-on-one time, if you know what I mean."

"You're such a matchmaker," Malik said as he came up for air, but he didn't move his arm from around Peyton's waist.

"And it's a good thing that I am," Theresa said, and nodded at Peyton's top button, which had sprung loose.

Malik immediately released her and Peyton buttoned her top. "If you two lovebirds are finished, we need your help cleaning up."

"Aye, aye, sir." Malik saluted her and turned to Peyton. "Sorry about that."

"Don't be sorry." Peyton leaned over and brushed her lips across his. "I wanted you to kiss me."

"Really?" Malik whispered. "Because there's more where that came from."

"Down boy." Peyton patted his shoulder.

"We'll have to pick this up another time," Malik commented.

They returned to the dining hall and found most of the crowd had dispersed and the volunteer crew was cleaning up. They pitched in and wiped down tables and washed dishes. Afterwards, they sat down and took a breather.

"Whew!" Malik said. "I'm beat." After working all day and volunteering this evening, he was exhausted.

"Me too." Peyton plopped down beside him.

"How about we go on an official date tomorrow night?" Malik asked.

"I'd like that," Peyton said, smiling. She wanted to move forward with her life. "What do you have planned?"

"Leave that up to me," Malik said. "I'll take care of all the details. Just be ready for me."

Was there a sexual overtone to his directive? Peyton wondered. "Oh I'll be ready," she replied.

Chapter 5

The next evening Peyton was more than ready. Surprisingly, she wasn't nervous at the prospect of spending time with Malik that night. She welcomed it. When the doorbell rang, Peyton buzzed Malik up to her apartment.

"Hey." Peyton swung open the door. "Come on in." Peyton pulled him inside. He was looking ruggedly handsome, dressed in a royal-blue dress shirt, black slacks and a black leather bomber jacket.

"You look great," Malik said. His eyes roved over her and feasted on the burgundy silk wrap dress that emphasized her slender waist, accompanied by strappy sandals. When his eyes finally gazed into Peyton's, he nearly lost it. The minimal makeup and the luxuriously big curls made her look sexy as hell. "Let's go. Otherwise I won't be responsible for my actions," Malik rasped huskily.

Peyton grinned. She understood because she'd felt it too, an underlying current of sexual tension.

"I hope you're in the mood for a fusion between Southern and Latin food, along with some good jazz," Malik asked.

"Why's that?" Peyton asked once they were out of the door.

"Because the place I'm taking you to has a Southern-Caribbean-African influence."

"New York is all new to me. So I'm sure I'll love wherever you take me," Peyton responded honestly.

Malik led her out to his BMW, which was usually housed in his garage. He lived so close to the community center in Harlem, he took the train or he could walk. But since Peyton lived in Brooklyn, a car was a necessity.

When they arrived at the Riverbank State Park, Malik pulled up right outside the restaurant and a valet parked his car. The River Room had an expansive pyramid-shaped ceiling, rectangular and circular wall motifs in alternating green, gold, fuchsia and indigo colors. Peyton enjoyed the supper club feel and the view of the George Washington Bridge.

"This place is great," Peyton said enthusiastically. "Thanks for bringing me."

"It was my pleasure." Malik said. He took charge and ordered a bottle of sauvignon blanc with his Caribbean crab cakes, while Peyton ordered the spiced duck with collard greens and sweet potato puree.

After their delicious meal, they enjoyed the soulful sounds of a solo singer-keyboardist. During the set, Malik scooted his chair back and rose to his feet. "Let's dance." Several couples had already taken to the floor.

"All right." Peyton slid her hand into his.

Once they were on the dance floor, Malik slid his arms around her waist and Peyton circled her arms around his neck and together they swayed to the music. Malik used the opportunity to nuzzle her earlobe. He couldn't decipher what scent Peyton was wearing. All he knew was that she smelled fragrant and deliciously sweet.

When Malik's rock-hard chest came into contact with her, an electrifying shudder reverberated right through Peyton. He must have felt it too, because when she glanced up he rewarded her with a smile, and a sensuous light passed between them. They danced to several songs, before the band changed to some up-tempo music.

After they'd listened to a couple of jazz sets, Malik suggested a walk along the pier.

"That sounds great." Peyton accepted Malik's hand.

They walked in silence for what seemed like ages, listening to the sounds of nature, when Malik broached a subject that had been on his mind.

"How long were you married?" Malik asked out of the blue.

Peyton was shocked, even though she shouldn't be. It was a logical question. He had to be curious about her past. "A little over seven years."

"Long time," Malik commented at her side.

"Does that bother you?" Peyton asked. "That I've been married before?"

"No, not really." Malik shook his head. "It's just hard for me to imagine that kind of love and devotion."

"Haven't you ever been in love?" Peyton asked, stopping their walk. She knew that love was a beautiful thing with the right person.

"No," Malik replied, turning to Peyton. "There were moments I thought I was—was *sure* I was—but looking back, I know I wasn't. Sometimes I wonder if I'm capable of loving another person."

Peyton wondered what would make Malik say that.

"I think you are. You're such an amazingly kind and giving person, you have the capacity to love, Malik. You've already shown you can. You just have to allow yourself to."

"You really think so?" Malik asked.

Peyton nodded.

A nervous knot formed in Peyton's stomach when Malik's brown eyes focused on hers in the moonlight. And when he finally grabbed both sides of her face and swooped down and captured her lips, Peyton thought she'd died and gone to heaven. Winding her arms around his back, Peyton drank in the sweetness of his kiss and sunk into his embrace.

Malik buried his hands in her thick hair and crushed her to him. His lips weren't hard, they were surprisingly gentle. Raising his mouth from hers, Malik gazed into her eyes before his lips descended over hers with an urgency and mastery Peyton had never felt.

"I want you so much, Peyton," Malik whispered against her lips.

"I want you too," Peyton responded, "but I'm not sure I'm ready."

"Nothing has to happen tonight, Peyton." When she looked down he tilted her chin upward so she could look at him. "There's no pressure here. We will make love when you're ready." He sealed his comment with another mind-blowing kiss that left Peyton weak at the knees and wondering why she was holding back.

Slowly, they made their way to the valet to pick up Malik's car. On the drive to her apartment, Peyton was a nervous wreck. There was no mistaking the undisguised desire that flared in Malik's eyes. And although she wanted him as much as he wanted her, Peyton was nervous about a night with Malik.

If the way he kissed and caressed her was any indication, he had a lot of experience pleasing a woman. She'd only been with David. Their sex life had been mutually pleasurable, but David never set her afire the way Malik did. Just one touch or one look from him would send her mind reeling and her pulse spinning. She could only imagine what it would feel like when they made love for the first time.

When the car stopped, Peyton swallowed hard. *Here goes.*

"Is everything okay?" Malik asked when Peyton didn't make a move to exit the vehicle. He could sense her nervousness on the drive home. Perhaps she was regretting her decision. He intended to take things slow and easy. He was aware that Peyton hadn't been with another man since her husband's death. He wanted to reassure her that there was nothing she could ever do that would make him not want her.

"Yes, I'm fine." Peyton squeezed her hands together tightly.

"Trust me," Malik said, before stepping out of the car and coming to open her door.

Once he said those two words, Peyton knew that she did and that she had nothing to fear. Malik was a kind and giving man and he would be the same kind of lover. She took his proffered hand and together they climbed the stairs to her apartment.

Once inside, Peyton turned on the hall light. They stared at each other for a long time before Malik lifted her off her feet and carried her to the bedroom. All they had was the moonlight streaming in from the window, and that was all they needed.

Malik lowered her to the floor, and as he did, her breasts crushed against him and he felt the hardened peaks of her nipples graze his chest. Malik couldn't resist driving his hands through her glossy black hair, and when he did, Peyton sighed as if he was already inside her. "I want you so much, Peyton," Malik whispered huskily. "Do you want me?" He needed to hear the words.

"I do," Peyton replied, nodding. "I want you to make love to me." Desire was throbbing deep inside her and she wanted to belong to Malik in every way. She wrapped her arms around his neck and brought his head towards hers. His lips covered hers hungrily as he both gave and sought pleasure. She returned his deep kiss and welcomed the sweeping thrusts of his tongue inside her mouth. She ran her fingers through his dreads, and held his head in place as a silent plea for him to continue.

Malik groaned and pulled her closer until their bodies were aligned and she could feel him, hard and throbbing against her. Liquid heat pooled inside her belly and Peyton whimpered. "Malik, please." Malik honored her request and released the tie on her wrap dress. She felt the warmth of his hands on her back and the coolness of the air as her dress slid down her body. Despite herself, Peyton trembled.

As she stood in front of him, wearing only a lacy bra and matching thong, Malik groaned and his eyes raked her from head to toe. Peyton was so beautiful, and he was eager to see all of her.

As he admired her, Peyton nervously reached behind her and unhooked her bra and let it drop to the floor. She watched as his gaze focused on her bare breasts, but she didn't let nervousness stop her. She slid her panties down her legs, stepped out of them and kicked them to the side until she was standing completely naked in front of him. Peyton had never done that before, she'd always let David take the lead. But it was different with Malik. It felt right.

"You're absolutely gorgeous." Malik let out a ragged breath at the sight of Peyton and reached out to cup her small but firm breasts. As he brushed the nipples with his forefingers, they grew hot and heavy in his hands.

Malik couldn't resist dipping down for a taste. He took the tight bud in his mouth and her unique scent filled his senses. He flicked and teased it with his tongue until her pelvis began to undulate against him. He grabbed ahold of her buttocks and held her firmly against his painful erection and suckled her relentlessly. When she moaned for more, all thought and reason left Malik and he swiftly threw off his jacket and unbuttoned his shirt.

Peyton heard the snap of his pants seconds before they, along with his shirt and underwear, hit the floor in quick succession. She ran her fingertips down his chiseled chest and firm abs. "You're simply magnificent," she said and bent down to flick her tongue across his nipple. When Malik groaned, Peyton smiled and moved over to tease the other nipple with equal ardor.

Malik grabbed for her and they tumbled onto the bed in a mass of limbs. When Peyton wrapped her legs around him, Malik knew he had to slow down the pace, otherwise it would be over too fast, and he wanted their first encounter to be special, not quick and hurried.

"Easy, baby," Malik whispered in her ear.

Peyton blushed. "I'm sorry…I'm not usually…so…" "Wanton" was the word she was looking for, but she couldn't think of it. The tempest of desire swirling inside her was undeniable. She'd seen his swollen, throbbing member and she was ready for him.

He cupped her chin in his hand and tilted her head

to look at him. "It's okay. I'm glad to see you're as eager as I am."

Malik brought his lips down gently upon hers, tasting her and drinking her in. Her lips were soft, warm and moist as they opened to his searching tongue. She tasted like heaven, and Malik knew he wanted more, much more. He caressed her narrow waist and showered it with kisses.

His hands continued their journey, sliding first to caress the softness of her thighs before moving higher to cup her intimately. He slowly stroked her feminine nub with his thumb, lazily circling it. Then he eased a finger slowly inside. She was hot and wet around him and it turned him on immensely.

"Oh, Malik." Peyton sighed. Malik loved that she called his name out while in the throes of an orgasm, so he continued slipping his finger in and out while his thumb teased her already sensitive core.

Peyton's body bucked upward from the bed and Malik understood. It was time to taste her sweet nectar. Before Peyton could realize his intent, he'd inserted his tongue where his long, narrow fingers had been and began teasing and stroking her with swift flicks. Peyton moaned uncontrollably and it didn't take long for tremors to engulf her entire body.

And yet he still wanted more. As Malik looked down at Peyton in the moonlight, he was amazed at how beautiful she was and that they were finally together. Tonight had been a culmination of intense longing that began the moment he'd met her, and now he would have his heart's desire.

Malik went for a condom out of his pants pocket, but Peyton beat him to it by pulling one out of her night-stand drawer and handing it to him. Malik smiled.

Malik rolled a condom over the length of him and then eased Peyton onto her back and gently parted her legs. His erection, hot and heavy, glided into her silken heat. Her eyelids fluttered shut and her entire body quivered as Malik entered her.

She was warm and tight, and Malik had to remind himself to take it slow, even though his body wanted a quick release. It had been a long time since Peyton had been intimate, so he needed to pace himself, but that was hard to do because Peyton was already moving beneath him.

When Malik grasped her hands and intertwined them with his above her head, their bodies ground together in perfect unison as though they were one. Peyton realized she had never felt this fulfilled, this complete. Ever. She wrapped her legs around Malik's waist and matched his every thrust by undulating her hips. With every thrusting motion, she moaned and Malik became ignited. He pushed against her one last time, and when the crescendo came they both fell over the edge together.

"Are you okay?" he asked, rolling to his side and glancing at Peyton. He wasn't so sure *he* was. The aftershocks were still rippling through his body.

"Why? Do I not seem fine?" Peyton inquired, even though her breathing was rapid and she was flushed.

"No, it was just that…" Malik was at a loss.

"It was incredible for me too," Peyton said, stroking his stubbly jaw. "I hope I satisfied you."

Malik laughed. "Are you kidding? Couldn't you tell? You satisfied me in every way imaginable, Peyton. You were wonderful." And he was ready for round two. But as he cuddled closer, Peyton's heavy-lidded eyes closed shut. *There's always tomorrow,* Malik thought.

* * *

The next morning, Peyton awoke to sunlight streaming through her window. She glanced over to her side, but the bed was empty. Rising, she slipped on her lavender satin robe and glanced down the hallway. She found the apartment empty and no sign of Malik. *Where has he gone?* she asked herself, just as he came through the door carrying two Starbucks cups and a bag. Still wearing his tailored trousers and dress shirt, Malik looked sexy as hell. Peyton was sure every woman he'd encountered was wondering whose bed he'd come out of and wishing she'd been the recipient.

"Whatcha got there?" Peyton asked, walking towards him.

"I remembered you liked lattes, so I took the liberty of getting one for you." Malik handed her a cup and headed to the kitchen, adding, "Along with picking up some bagels and cream cheese."

"Thank you," Peyton smiled at his thoughtfulness as she followed behind him.

Malik wasn't surprised to find Peyton's kitchen in meticulous condition, as the lady herself liked everything in its proper place. He opened the cabinets and searched for some plates.

"Second cabinet to your left," Peyton said, taking a seat at the breakfast bar.

Malik busied himself by taking out bagels for himself and Peyton. He felt somewhat awkward in the morning light. Usually after his relationships took the next logical step, Malik didn't stick around. For the first time, he wasn't in a hurry to leave; he actually wanted to stay.

"So, what do you have planned for today?" Malik inquired.

"Research, research and research," Peyton answered,

tearing open a bagel. As she lathered the cream cheese on, she knew that wasn't what he meant. "Did you have something else in mind?" Peyton bit into the bagel.

Malik grinned mischievously. "I do, but after breakfast."

Chapter 6

Peyton stared out of the window in her office. Her mind kept replaying the images of her and Malik in bed together all weekend long. The way he'd touched her, the way he'd made her feel. She hadn't even recognized the sexual creature she'd become with him.

"Ahem." A cough came from behind her. Peyton turned around and found Amber smiling at her. "Looks like someone was in another world."

"I was," Peyton admitted.

"Anyplace special?"

"What do you mean?"

When Amber looked Peyton straight in the eye, Peyton couldn't resist smiling broadly. "Peyton, you are glowing like a kid on Christmas morning. Did you and Malik take your relationship to the next level?"

"Okay, you caught me. I'm busted." Peyton couldn't

lie. "We did. And it was fantastic!" Peyton sighed dramatically.

"See, I told you there was nothing to worry about," Amber replied. "It was just like riding a bike."

Peyton thought back to a moment when she was on top of Malik and was riding him until they both came, shattering in a million tiny pieces. "I wouldn't describe it as riding a bike, but it did all come back to me." Peyton grinned. "And I'm looking forward to another spin."

"I bet. It's just really good to see you like this, Peyton. When you said you were moving here, Jude and I were concerned. But it looks like our fears were unfounded. You're thriving, girlfriend."

"I think New York was just what I needed," Peyton said. She felt as if she'd come out of a dense fog. She hadn't felt this way in years, and it felt amazing. "Malik is a wonderful man."

"Well, don't fall too quickly," Amber warned. "This is your first real relationship since David died. You need to shop around the block first. You know, see what's out there."

"I've seen what's out there, Amber, and it's not all it's cracked up to be. What's your problem? I thought you liked Malik."

"I do," Amber replied. "But sometimes the first man you meet isn't always the right one. Sometimes he's the catalyst to propel you into your next relationship."

"I don't know. Malik is pretty close to perfection," Peyton joked.

"All right." Amber knew when to let a matter drop.

"Care to give me some more advice on how I can get through to one of my students?"

"Are we talking about the single mother?"

Peyton nodded. "I met with her and her boyfriend to

explain our program and how volunteering would bene-fit her, but it didn't go over very well. And to make matters worse, Kendra didn't show up for class today."

"So what are you going to do?" Amber asked, leaning against the desk.

"I thought I'd call and check on her. You know? Make sure everything's all right." Peyton had a nagging feeling in the pit of her stomach that something was wrong.

"I don't think that's a good idea," Amber replied. "Students miss class, Peyton. This isn't high school."

"I know," Peyton said. "But that doesn't mean I don't care." Many times she'd seen her mother, Lydia Allen, make a home visit if she suspected a student was in trou-ble. Peyton had always admired that about her and she was following her example.

"Okay," Amber said. "Do as you please, but if you want my advice, I say steer clear. I've got to get going. I have a six o'clock I need to prepare for." And with that, Amber was out the door.

Peyton disagreed, and once Amber had gone, she immediately dialed Kendra, who picked up after several rings. "Hello."

"Kendra, this is Professor Sawyer. You weren't in class today. I thought I'd call."

"Well…uh…" Kendra stammered. She hadn't ex-pected a personal phone call from her professor at home. "Tamara was sick and I had to stay home and take care of her."

Peyton didn't believe that for a moment. She suspected Omar was the reason she'd missed class. "Kendra, what's going on?"

"I told you, the baby was sick."

"All right, so you'll be in class on Wednesday?"

"Yes, I'll be there." Kendra quickly hung up the phone.

Peyton was worried. Something was definitely going on and she intended to find out what.

"How are things between you and the professor?" Dante asked when Malik strolled into his restaurant for lunch.

"Things couldn't be better, Dante," Malik replied, grinning. Now that he and Peyton had finally become lovers, everything was as it should be. "Peyton and I are finally on track."

"So when's the wedding?" Dante joked as he dried off several glasses.

"Slow down," Malik said. "You should be asking Q that question, not me." Q and Avery were inseparable these days, as evidenced by the fact that they'd even ambushed him together. "Peyton and I are in the 'getting to know each other' stage. We are nowhere near marriage. I doubt she'd be ready to take that step anyway."

"Why would you say that?"

"She was married before and her husband died in a car accident."

"That's terrible."

"Yeah," Malik said, nodding. "So she won't be ready to jump the broom anytime soon."

"Which is music to your ears," Dante replied. Malik didn't fool him for a moment. Say the word "commitment" and he went scurrying in the other direction.

"You know my opinion on the subject of marriage."

"You came in walking on air. You mark my words, Malik, you'll be eating those words," Dante predicted. "And I for one am going to laugh my butt off."

Peyton took a taxi over to Kendra's residence in the Bronx later that afternoon. She didn't know what she was going to do when she got there; Peyton just knew she had to try something.

When she arrived at Kendra's address, the taxi driver looked back at her. "Are you sure you want me to drop you off here?" he asked, looking around. This sure didn't look like the place a classy lady such as Peyton should be.

She glanced around the lower-income neighborhood. "Yes, but can you do me a favor? Stay for fifteen? I won't be long." As an added incentive, Peyton handed him a twenty.

The taxi driver thought about it for a moment. He'd hate to see her stranded, so he nodded. "Fifteen minutes is all you got. After that, I'm gone."

"Thanks." Peyton hopped out of the car. She walked up to the buzzer and was about to press it when a resident came out, so Peyton slipped inside. The apartment building was old and rundown, but Peyton didn't let that deter her. She climbed the squeaky stairs to the third floor. When she found apartment 203, Peyton knocked on the door.

When Kendra opened the door, she was shocked to find Peyton on the other side. "Professor Sawyer, what are you doing here?" she blurted out.

Peyton stared back at her student and her heart went out to her. One of Kendra's eyes was black and blue, even though she had tried to cover it with makeup. *Had Omar struck her?*

"When you didn't come to class, I decided to come see for myself—and I'm glad I did." Peyton pushed herself inside the apartment. She found Kendra's six-month-old daughter cooing in a nearby bassinet. The baby looked perfectly healthy. Peyton spun around and faced Kendra. "So you lied."

Kendra hung her head low. "I'm sorry."

"Why?" Peyton asked. "Has Omar said or done something to you?"

"Why would you ask that?" Kendra replied defensively.

"Kendra, you look terrible."

"Do I really look that bad?" Kendra rushed over to the hall mirror.

"I've seen the signs before," Peyton replied. She'd been to enough shelters to recognize a battered woman. "What happened?"

"I tried, Professor Sawyer." Kendra's voice broke. "I tried to come and volunteer, but Omar caught me on my way out after I'd told him I wouldn't go, and he got really angry."

"Did he hit you, Kendra?"

"He didn't mean to. It was an accident," Kendra explained. "I tried to move past him and he accidentally struck me in the face. He didn't mean to, Dr. Sawyer. Omar loves me."

Peyton nodded. "Kendra, I'm not sure if it's safe for you here. You should come with me. I can take you to a shelter."

"So me and my baby can be homeless?" Kendra shook her head. "No, thank you, Dr. Sawyer. I know you mean well, but I think it best if you go."

"I couldn't agree more," Omar said from the doorway. "I think it's time you left, Professor, especially if you want to keep that taxi that's waiting downstairs."

Shocked, Peyton rose to her feet and glanced at her watch. Her fifteen minutes were nearly up. She'd come to talk some common sense into Kendra, but today was not going to be her lucky day. Omar's presence was looming. Peyton knew when to toss in the towel, at least for now. "I took the liberty of contacting one of my students, and they were kind enough to copy their notes from today's lecture." She handed Kendra a manila envelope.

Kendra glanced at Omar as if she needed approval to accept the package from Peyton. He nodded, so Kendra took the envelope. "Thanks, that's real kind of you, Professor Sawyer."

"No problem. I'll see you in class." Peyton gave Kendra a halfhearted smile and turned on her heel. She flew out the door, and she was nearly down the hall when Omar caught up with her at the landing.

"Don't come here again, Professor," Omar said, walking towards Peyton.

"I came here to help Kendra." Peyton would not be intimidated by some twenty-year-old abuser. "And I will continue to do that, Omar, whether you like it or not."

Omar pointed a finger at Peyton. "Don't say I didn't warn you." He turned his back on her and went back inside the apartment.

Peyton rushed down the stairs in the nick of time. "Thanks for waiting," she said when she reached the safety of the taxi's interior.

"You're welcome," the driver replied.

Later that afternoon, Malik reviewed the center's financials. After his interview appeared in *Manhattan Weekly,* he'd expected offers to come poring in, but all he'd had was a few small donations. Sure, he appreciated those, but he still needed a large donation. Malik was tallying the donations when he was paged to reception. It was probably one of the parents from the center or someone from the community. With his open-door policy, Malik was used to unexpected visitors.

He rushed through the double doors. A man's back was to him, so Malik walked forward and touched his shoulder. "May I help you?" he asked.

Malik was ill-prepared when the man turned around.

Malik stared into the darkest, coldest eyes he'd ever encountered, he was standing face-to-face with his stepfather, Joe Johnson.

Chapter 7

Even though time had aged Joe with lines, wrinkles and a receding hairline, Malik would never forget the evil bastard's face. Except that now Joe Johnson no longer intimidated him. Malik wasn't the same nine-year-old who'd quivered in the corner of a closet hoping Joe wouldn't find him. He not only equaled Johnson in physique, he was also several inches taller.

"Malik, it's good to see you." Joe extended his hand as if Malik would shake it. Instead, Malik glared at him.

Joe continued speaking. "I saw the humanitarian article about you in the *Manhattan Weekly* and heard you needed a corporate sponsor."

Malik found his voice. "And why would what *I* need matter to you?" He hadn't heard a word from Joe or his mother after they'd failed to show up for the hearing that would place him permanently in child protective services. His own mother had wiped her hands clean of him when he was only ten years old, because that's what Joe Johnson had wanted. Several years ago, he heard she'd died of cervical cancer. He'd been so angry at her for all the hurt she'd allowed to be inflicted on him that he hadn't attended the funeral, all because of this man.

Malik's mind sprang back to an incident that had happened when he was nine years old and had stayed out after dark. When he returned, Joe punched him in his face and blood had poured out of his nose and lips. He'd lived in constant fear and loneliness. He wanted to die at first, but thankfully the law had stepped in. He guessed that after too many black eyes, broken arms and hand prints around his neck where Joe had choked him into submission, there had been enough evidence for his teachers to call Department of Children's Services.

"I thought my company, Johnson Construction, might be able to help you out. As you can see, I've done quite well for myself." Joe motioned to the tailored slacks, blazer and Rolodex watch he was wearing.

"I don't *want* nor do I need any help from you."

"Oh c'mon, Williams." Joe circled Malik. "I see it like this. I help you." He poked Malik in the chest. "By renovating this dump for free and in turn you give me all future construction work at the community centers. It's a win-win situation."

Fury boiled inside Malik's veins and he thought he would explode. "Do you honestly think I'd ever accept anything from you?"

"No, but your center is in desperate need of money, isn't it?" Joe asked testily. "Well…I can help."

"I would never let a wife-beater and a child-abuser anywhere near this center. Now get out!" Malik yelled and pointed to the door. "And don't ever come back."

"How dare you talk to me like that, you little snot-nosed punk?" Joe took a threatening step towards Malik.

"Don't even try it, Joe," Malik warned. His eyes were as cold as steel as he spoke. "You're not the man you once were, and if you ever lay another hand on me, I promise you it will be your last move."

"So you're all high and mighty, now that you're over this center. Well, I remember when you were nothing but a crying little wuss begging for his mama to save him and I had to teach you a lesson."

Malik had heard enough and lunged at Joe shoving him up against the wall.

"Ohmigod!" Malik heard Loretta gasp from behind him, but he didn't care. He held his arm firmly up against Joe's throat, restricting his air passage. He'd waited a lifetime to show Joe Johnson what he was made of, and there was no time like the present. When Joe began to fight, Malik squeezed down harder.

Suddenly, Andrew walked through the center doors. When he saw Malik choking the man, he rushed over and pulled Malik off, but Malik lunged for Joe again.

"Malik, what's going on?" Andrew kept a firm grasp around Malik's arms. He hadn't seen Malik act this way since his youth, when he'd been an angry and distant young man. Back then, he'd been prone to getting into fights with the center's youth for no apparent reason. The only person that had been able to talk any sense into him back then had been Andrew. What had changed?

"This is the bastard that beat up me and my mother!" Malik shouted. "And I want him out of here now, or I swear, Andrew, I'm going to hurt him. And hurt him bad."

Andrew turned to the man who was still holding his

throat. "I ought to sue you for assault," Joe growled in Malik's face.

"Try it!" Malik took a menacing step towards Joe.

"You need to take hold of that young man." Joe clutched his throat. "He's out of control. I came here today to help. I offered to renovate this center free of charge and he attacked me without cause."

"Oh, I'm sure he had cause, Mr. Johnson." Andrew was well aware of who he was.

"How do you know my name?"

"Your reputation precedes you," Andrew stated. "I think it's best if you go. Leave your name and number with the receptionist and we'll review your offer."

"Thank you." Joe bowed his head, then sauntered over to Loretta, scribbled his info and quickly left the building.

Once he was no longer within range, Andrew released Malik.

"What did you say that for?" Malik asked, turning around and confronting Andrew. He had no right to speak for the center.

"What do you mean?"

"You said we'd review his offer," Malik replied. "When hell freezes over!"

"Malik, you've been looking for sponsors for months now, and the CAN board has already turned you down. Perhaps Joe is here to right the wrongs he's done."

Malik ran his fingers through his dreads. He couldn't believe what he was hearing. Andrew of all people should understand Malik's anger because he'd been on the receiving end of it during his adolescence. "That's bull and you know it, Andrew. Joe only cares about himself and what's in it for him. I will not let that man anywhere near this center, so he can terrorize innocent women and children. I swear if he comes in here again, I'll…"

Andrew grabbed Malik by the arm and pushed him towards the door. "Let's talk outside."

"I don't have anything else to say." Malik snatched his arm away and stormed off. "The subject is closed," he shouted over his shoulder. Seconds later the swinging double doors closed behind him.

"You did what?" Malik asked later that night when he and Peyton were snuggled on her couch watching movies and eating popcorn. He pushed away and looked at her like she had suddenly arrived from Mars. "What were you thinking, going to that area by yourself?"

He'd already had a hard enough day seeing Joe Johnson after twenty years, he didn't need to hear that the woman he was seeing was putting herself in harm's way unnecessarily.

"I was trying to help my student," Peyton said, defending her actions. She didn't care for Malik's tone. "Or at least I thought I was. But then her boyfriend came bursting in all big and bad. That's when I knew I'd made a gross miscalculation, so I retreated."

"Peyton, you should never have put yourself in that situation to begin with. It was dangerous. If you think her boyfriend is capable of hitting Kendra, imagine what he could have done to you? You've put yourself smack dab in the middle of a volatile situation…" Malik hugged Peyton close. The thought that something could have happened to her made him feel powerless and he hated that feeling. He felt as if he were a child all over again and he never wanted to feel that way, ever.

"I'm sorry, Malik." Peyton saw the fear in his eyes. She hadn't realized how deep his feelings for her went until now. He was genuinely worried for her well-being.

Peyton allowed Malik to hold her because it felt good. She'd missed the security that came with being held in a man's arms.

She hadn't realized the danger she was in until after she'd left Kendra's building. Omar could have gone psycho on her and she would have had no one to blame but herself. Perhaps Amber had been right all along. Maybe she *was* getting in too deep.

"Promise me you won't ever do something like that again."

"I promise."

Malik sighed. "Good. Now as for Kendra, it's clear this girl needs some help, but this time I'll talk to her—and on neutral territory. Say, after your next class."

"You would do that?"

"Of course. Don't you know you've got me wrapped around your little finger?"

"If I do," Peyton said, snuggling closer to Malik and teasing his earlobe with the tip of her tongue, "why don't you tell me what else has got you so upset?"

"There's nothing wrong."

"C'mon, Malik," Peyton said, kissing his neck. "I know something is bothering you. Why don't you tell me what it is. Did you have a bad day? Maybe I could fix it."

"You could say that," Malik replied, then turned stone-faced.

Why was it so hard for Malik to talk about his feelings? Peyton was willing to share her past and her story with him. What was it going to take for him to let her in? She paused from her teasing movements to look Malik in the eye. "I'm waiting…"

"Andrew and I had a disagreement over a sponsor for the center. His name is Joe Johnson and he's a real piece of work."

"Not again," Peyton replied. He'd already turned down Richard King's offer, and now another company. Peyton didn't understand his logic. "Malik, if the man is trying to help the center, you should consider him. If you're looking for perfection, I doubt you're going to find it."

"This man represents everything I'm against, Peyton."

"What do you mean?" She was confused.

"He's just someone I used to know," Malik said, rising from the couch.

"What aren't you telling me, Malik?" Peyton inquired. "Who is this man to you?"

"Can't you just drop it?" Malik said. "I'm sorry I even brought it up." Malik pushed away from her and stormed to the bathroom. She had no idea who Joe Johnson was and what he'd done to him, and Malik was in no way ready to share his past. He'd come a long way from that scared little nine-year-old boy, and he wanted the past to remain buried.

Andrew stopped Malik the following day, just as he was locking up his office.

"I'm busy right now, Andrew," Malik said. "Your lecture is going to have wait."

"No can do." Andrew stood in his path.

Seeing that he was several inches taller than Malik, and that that he respected Andrew, Malik acquiesced.

"Fine." Malik opened the door. "Say what you have to say, but my mind is not going to be changed on this subject." Malik motioned for Andrew to enter.

Andrew came inside his office and sat down. "Listen, son."

Malik rolled his eyes upward. Whenever Andrew called him "son," Malik knew he was in for a lecture.

"I know what this man did to you. I know how he hurt you and your mother, but this could be good for the center."

"I am not thirteen anymore, Andrew," Malik replied. "This man didn't just steal my Packman. It goes much deeper. The man physically abused me for years."

"Don't you think it's time to heal those wounds?" Andrew asked.

"That's not the reason Joe is here, Andrew. If he'd come here admitting the things he'd done and asking for forgiveness it *might* have made a difference, but he didn't. He came here with his chest all puffed out, acting like he was doing me a favor."

"Does it really matter, if the center benefits?"

"That's easy for you to say," Malik replied. "You didn't live through what I lived through."

"Oh, God, Malik." Andrew slid his fingers through his short salt-and-pepper Afro. "I'm not trying to downplay what happened to you. No one deserves the type of abuse that you and your mother endured at Joe Johnson's hands. But Joe is offering to do the work for free. Maybe he's changed."

Malik rose. "I've heard everything you've said, Andrew, and you know I love you. You've been not only a mentor to me, but a father figure. And I respect you greatly, but my mind is made up. *I* am the director of HCC, not you, and if that man shows his face here, he will be shown the door."

Andrew's shoulders sagged as he stood and headed for the door. "Thank you for hearing me out." Malik nodded and followed Andrew out and relocked his door.

Boom. Boom. Boom. Malik's fists hit the punching bag in quick succession at the Harlem YMCA later that evening.

"Easy there," Dante said. He was holding the bag and Malik was punching it like there was no tomorrow. Any second his veins were going to pop out of his temples.

"Sorry, man." Malik eased back on his heels for a few minutes before throwing two double jabs.

"All right," Dante said, stepping away from the bag, "what's going on?"

Malik hung his head. "Nothing's wrong, Dante. Don't punk out. Just hold the bag."

Dante threw off his gloves and walked away. Ever since they'd arrived Malik had been punishing him. First, he'd insisted on running for thirty minutes, forty-five minutes of weights and now boxing. Had he known that he was in a foul mood, Dante would have passed on the workout. His body was crying out for a hot shower. Although he kept himself fit and lean by eating right, he was nowhere near a fitness buff as Quentin and Malik, who constantly visited the gym.

"Dante, wait!" Malik jogged behind him. "I'm sorry, okay? I was having a bad day and I took it out on you." Ever since that sleazy scuzzball had come into the center a couple of days ago, he had not had a good night's sleep. It was like he was reliving his childhood all over again, but this time in his dreams.

He'd even begged off staying over at Peyton's last night. She'd already tried to pry the truth out of him, but Malik didn't want to talk about it with anyone. He'd closed that chapter of his life, or so he thought, until Joe Johnson showed up.

"Ya think?" Dante asked, pivoting on his heel and turning to face him.

"Something happened a couple of days ago that rattled me," Malik confided. "Actually, I should say *someone*."

"Who?"

"Joe Johnson."

The name was a blast from the past. "Your stepfather?"

"The one and only. Apparently his construction company is doing well, so he came to yank my chain by offering to renovate the center in exchange for me giving his company all future construction work at my centers."

"I can't believe he had the gall to act like he'd be doing you a favor," Dante replied.

"You're telling me." Malik wiped the sweat off his face with a towel. "And then Andrew had the nerve to get on my case and tell me I should accept his offer, when he knows how much I hate the man."

"What did you do?" Dante was almost afraid to ask.

"I nearly choked him half to death before Andrew stopped me. I warned Joe to never darken the center's doorstep. But I have a feeling I haven't seen the last of him."

Chapter 8

Malik dropped in on Friday, just as Peyton's class was ending. He hated that they hadn't been able to reconnect the other night. It wasn't like he didn't want her, but bringing up Joe Johnson had touched a raw nerve. He was hoping to make it up to her by helping her student, Kendra.

As the students exited, Malik slipped in. He glanced at Peyton, who nodded towards Kendra who was heading towards the door. At least Peyton smiled at him, which meant she wasn't too upset about his rude behavior the other evening.

Peyton was relieved when Kendra had come to class. Kendra sat in the back of the hall and had remained silent throughout her lecture. She wasn't sure if Omar had retaliated against the poor girl because of her surprise visit.

"Kendra, could you please wait a moment," Peyton called out. Slowly, the young mother turned around.

"Kendra, I don't know if you remember Malik Williams." Peyton motioned Malik over. "He's the director of the community center."

Kendra nodded. "I do."

"Can you spare a few minutes?" Malik asked, coming towards her. "I'd really like to talk to you."

Kendra glanced at her watch. "I have another class in thirty minutes."

"I won't be long," Malik replied.

"All right," Kendra agreed and walked over to take a seat.

"Do you mind giving us some time alone?" Malik asked, glancing up at Peyton, who'd come over to join them. "I'd like to talk to Kendra in private."

"Oh, of course," Peyton replied. Although she wanted to be present, she respected Kendra's right to privacy. Seconds later, she was out of the room.

Malik sat down next to Kendra. "I'm sure you're wondering why I'm here."

"I have some idea. Professor Sawyer asked you talk to me about my boyfriend, probably to encourage me to leave him because he struck me by accident. Am I right?"

"Yes, but that's not the only reason, I'm here, Kendra…" Malik responded. "I'm here because I've been in your shoes."

"You have?" Kendra's forehead bunched into a frown.

It was rare for Malik to open up to anyone, including his friends, about the abuse he'd endured at Joe's hands, but if his story could help keep another woman or child from getting hurt like him and his mother, than he'd tell it—but only to her. "I have. You see, Kendra,

my stepfather used to hit me. No—let me correct that—
he used to beat me."

"No!" Kendra's hand flew to her mouth.

"I endured a great deal, Kendra, because I was a
child and I had nowhere to run and no one to turn to."

"What about your mother?"

"She acted as if it weren't happening, because he was
hitting her too.

"Kendra, you have to stop this cycle. What happens
to your daughter when she gets older? Do you want her
father to hit her too?"

"Omar would never do that!" Kendra argued. "He only
hit me once, maybe twice, and he didn't mean to do it."

Malik noticed how her story changed from one to two
hits. "Are you sure? Are you honestly willing to gamble
your daughter's future on a 'what if'?" he inquired.

"No, but what would you suggest I do? I'm dependent on Omar." Kendra's eyes welled up with tears.

"And he knows it." Malik struggled to keep his voice
calm. "But you don't have to stay, Kendra. You can get
out. There are many options available to you that
weren't there when my mother needed help. I'm begging you to please consider going to a friend or a shelter.
There's also financial support available to you if you just
apply. And if you're scared, you can take out a restraining order against him."

Kendra shook her head vehemently. "That's not
necessary."

"All right, then take these applications." Malik
reached in his portfolio and handed her several forms.
"They are applications for financial and childcare assistance, and there's a list of addresses of local women's
shelters. Consider what I've said, Kendra. I'd hate for
what happened to me to happen to your daughter."

"Thank you," Kendra said, squeezing Malik's hand, "for sharing your story with me."

Telling his story to Kendra was a lot different than trying to tell it to Peyton. "You can call me any time you want to talk." Malik reached in his wallet and pulled out his business card. "And in case of emergency, my cell number's on the back."

"Thanks, again." Kendra smiled tentatively and hurriedly left the room. She found Peyton outside the door. She nodded at her before leaving the building.

Peyton returned to the classroom and found Malik with a tortured expression on his face. Had Kendra said something to upset him? "Is everything okay?"

"Yeah, everything's fine," Malik lied, as images of his mother, bloodied and bruised on the kitchen floor, flashed through his mind. The sounds of her crying as Joe backhanded her echoed in Malik's head. A profound feeling of helplessness washed over Malik.

"And Kendra?"

"Uh…" Malik tried to clear his head of the negative pictures. "That girl's in harm's way. I just hope she makes the right decision before it's too late."

"Thank you so much." Peyton squeezed Malik as hard as she could. "I really appreciate your help."

"You're welcome." Malik returned the hug. She had no idea just how much he'd needed that hug. It had taken a lot for him to dredge up the memories, even if it was to do good.

On Saturday night, he and Peyton joined Quentin and Avery at a café on the Lower East Side to listen to poetry and have a few drinks. Peyton had encouraged Malik to meet with Quentin and show them there were no hard feelings, and he had agreed. Malik was doing everything he could to ease some of the tension that had arisen between him and Peyton since Joe's reappearance. They hadn't been intimate again since the night after The River Room, but Malik was hoping to remedy that.

"Hey, guys!" Malik walked in hand-in-hand with Peyton. They found Quentin and Avery already seated at a table.

"Malik." Quentin rose and shook his hand. "You're looking well." More than that, Malik seemed happy and it looked good on him.

"Hi," Peyton greeted them. "Good to see you again."

"You too." Avery smiled.

"What's new?" Malik asked, helping Peyton into her seat before seating himself.

"Well, I've just finished putting together an exhibit for Avery's gallery," Quentin said, sitting down.

"What's the name again?" Peyton vaguely remembered Malik mentioning it.

"It's the Henri Lawrence Gallery, in Soho," Avery answered. "The show is going to be attended by some major movers and shakers in New York." She was so excited that they'd finally gotten the exhibit off the ground. Her boss, Hunter Garrett, had thought Quentin had forgotten the idea after he'd brought it up several months ago, but Avery hadn't—and now she was seeing her hard work come to fruition. "You should come, Malik. You never know, there might be some prospects there."

The moment Avery brought up a corporate sponsor, conversation ceased. Malik glanced at Quentin as if he should keep his girlfriend in check.

Peyton knew Avery was only trying to help, so she spoke up. "Avery was only making a suggestion. And if you ask me, Richard King was the solution to your

problem. At least you'd know who you're dealing with."
Peyton exhaled. Beggars couldn't be choosers. Malik
was just too stubborn to see it.

"I couldn't agree with you more." Quentin supported
Peyton, much to Malik's dismay. "Despite your less than
enthusiastic response, Richard is still willing to donate
a significant contribution to the Harlem center."

"And how would you know that?" Malik queried,
glancing sideways at Quentin.

"Don't get all defensive." Quentin patted Malik's
shoulder. "We had dinner the other night and he asked
if HCC was still in need and I said yes."

Peyton touched Malik's arm. "Won't you at least
consider it? We all," Peyton nodded to Quentin and
Avery, "would be there to support you in this venture.
You are not in this alone."

Malik's head was spinning. No woman had ever
said that to him before. In the back of his mind, he
always knew he wasn't alone and that Quentin, Sage
and Dante were there for him. But it was nice to hear
the words aloud.

"And if you want the media involved in every step of
this," Avery continued, sensing that Peyton had gotten
through to Malik, "then we can have a camera crew on
board the moment Richard signs the check."

"Just think of what it would mean to the community,"
Quentin said. "Think of what it would have meant to us
growing up." When Malik lowered his head, Quentin
nodded to Peyton and Avery. They had sealed it.

Malik remembered all too well what it was like not
to have the latest equipment and games in the center.
Yet, somehow Andrew had made do. Couldn't he do the
same? *But you don't have to,* an inner voice spoke back.
He had the unique opportunity to take Andrew's dream

a step farther, if he only had the guts. *Am I really that much of a coward?* Perhaps Joe Johnson had been right.

"All right," Malik conceded and threw his hands in the air. "Okay. You guys have won me over."

"Whew!" Quentin wiped fake sweat of his brow. "You are a hard man to convince."

"True, but you have to admit that my apprehension had merit."

"Which you and Richard will address in a sit-down meeting," Quentin responded. "Pull all your requests together, my brother, because there's a center to renovate."

"To working together!" Peyton lifted her beer bottle.

"To working together." Malik smiled at her and clinked his bottle with the group.

"You're joking," Theresa said when Malik told her the news bright and early on Monday. "You're going to accept a contribution from the King Corporation?"

"Yes."

"Well, knock me over with a feather!" Theresa exclaimed. If anyone had ever told her that Malik Williams would accept a penny from Richard King she would have told them "when pigs fly!"

"What changed your mind?"

"You mean *'who?'*" Malik asked. "Peyton, Quentin and Avery all ganged up on me and I succumbed to the pressure."

"This is really great news. Just think of all the ways we can spend King's money." Theresa rubbed her hands together.

"Call a brainstorming session with all the department heads for tomorrow," Malik advised. "And get Blake Harris on the line." Malik was eager to show the president of CAN he'd procured the money on his own for the center. This would be quite a feather in his cap and would show CAN that they had not made a mistake when they appointed him.

"Sure thing, boss."

"Hey, stranger." Peyton kissed her brother on the cheek when she met him for a hot pastrami on rye at a local deli. With her brother's finances, they had to find cheap eats. "Where have you been hiding?"

"Me?" Jude exclaimed. "You're the one who's been too busy—first with your students and classes and then with some new man—whom I'd like to meet, by the way."

Peyton laughed. "Amber has a big mouth." Just that afternoon, Malik had texted her to say he was thinking about her and to make sure they were still on for this weekend—which she absolutely was.

"Well, someone had to tell me what's going on. Especially since my own sister can't be bothered."

Peyton felt instantly terrible. Jude was right. She had been neglecting her baby brother. "I'm sorry, Jude. What can I do to make it up to you?"

"Well, for starters you can come to my new Broadway show!" he announced.

"Get out!"

"That's right. It's just a small part, but it's Broadway."

"I am so proud of you," Peyton said, beaming. "And so will Mom and Dad." She'd watched Jude struggle to become an actor, and it wasn't an easy life, wondering when your next paycheck was coming; but Peyton admired the fact that Jude pursued his dreams. Her mother would have to begrudgingly admit it as well.

"I hope so."

"When does it open?"

"Friday. We've been in rehearsals the last couple of weeks."

Peyton reached across the table and grabbed Jude's hand. "This is wonderful news. Let's celebrate." Peyton looked around for the waitress. When she caught her eye, she motioned her over. "Two beers, please."

"I can't believe you're drinking in the middle of the afternoon."

"Oh, what the hell!" Peyton shrugged.

"What has gotten into you?" Jude asked. He hadn't seen Peyton this happy, this full of life, in a long time.

"I don't know, Jude. I guess for the first time in a long time I'm finally enjoying life again. And it feels darn good." After David died, she'd wanted to crawl up in a hole and die too. He had been her whole world.

"So what's this fella's name?"

"Malik Williams, not that you didn't already know." Jude grinned mischievously. "Tell me about him."

"He's director of community centers for the Children's Aid Network, but his home base is in Harlem."

"He sounds like just your type, philanthropic and completely altruistic."

"Is there something wrong with that?" Peyton inquired.

"Of course not," Jude replied. "He's just different from David." His brother-in-law had been much more into himself than into helping others, but Peyton had adored him since she was a preteen. "But in a good way."

Peyton breathed a huge sigh of relief. She wanted her family to like Malik. "We'll come to your opening and you can meet him and form your own opinion."

"I would love that, sis."

The brainstorming session was a free-for-all, with Malik and the center's business manager, Greg Burns, holding court. In light of the impending contribution, the volunteer director, Denise Burke, the programs director, Brad Edwards, the school director, Mary Parton and Karen Morgan of health services were all vying for funds. Theresa had even contacted Andrew to sit in on the meeting and contribute his expertise.

Malik stood up. "Hold your horses, everyone." He settled the troops down. "I know you all want a piece of the pie, but we have to prioritize. The center needs a makeover. That means new paint, carpet and new tile in the administrative offices, while the kitchen and the computer center will get brand-new equipment."

"What about the clinic?" Karen asked. "We can use some up-to-date equipment. You know how important free health and dental care is to the community. Maybe even expand our services to include vision exams."

"Get me a list of your top needs and we will address them," Malik replied. "That includes the rest of you." He pointed to the group.

"I will review your requests and come up with what I think is a reasonable number to present to the King Corporation. And since time is of the essence, please get it to me by the end of the week. Meeting adjourned."

After the group had dispersed, Andrew came up to Malik and shook his hand. "I'm proud of you, Malik."

Malik stepped back. "I'm surprised. You haven't been very much, these days."

Andrew sighed. "That's not true. I'm always proud of you, Malik. Even more so because you put your personal animosity towards Richard King on the shelf and did what was best for HCC. It's why I recommended you as my replacement years ago."

Malik smiled humbly. "Thank you, Andrew."

"Malik, you have a call on line one," Loretta announced, paging him over the intercom.

"If you'll excuse me, Andrew." Malik walked away. Despite the congratulations, there was still some distance between him and Andrew. Malik didn't know how to get back to the way things were before Joe entered the picture.

"Hello?" he asked, picking up the phone.

"Hey, handsome," Peyton said.

"What's up?"

"I'm calling to change our plans. My brother's show is opening on Friday and we've got to go."

"Of course." Malik loved a good Broadway show.

"Be ready tomorrow at nine, baby, because I'm picking you up," Peyton replied saucily. After he'd gone out of his way to help Kendra, Peyton was starting to fall hard for Malik Williams.

"I look forward to it."

Chapter 9

"Hey handsome." Peyton winked when Malik opened the door of his brownstone. He looked scrumptious in a classic pink dress shirt and grey trousers. Add the shoulder-length dreads and sexy stubble and he was a walking advertisement for sex.

Peyton strolled in and looked around. This was the first time she'd been to his place. For some reason, they were always at her apartment. She loved the hardwood floors and brick fireplace. The black-red-and-green color motif and African statues and masks were a reflection of Malik's personal style.

"You look sexy as hell!" Malik exclaimed. Peyton's long hair was pinned up in a French roll with several tendrils dangling on either side of her face. And the dress was another story entirely. Silver-toned beads detailed the V-neckline of Peyton's graphite-colored silk dress with chiffon overlay. The V dipped surprising low and allowed Malik a nice view of her cleavage. The design flattered her and made Malik want to rip it off. "Want a tour?" he asked—before he did just that. The least he could do was give her a tour of his abode so she could see another side to him, since he was so closed off on the subject of his past.

"Sure." Peyton followed Malik down the hall. His kitchen was very modern and masculine, with dark cherry-wood cabinets, stainless steel appliances and granite countertops. Down the hall, his office housed a large maple desk and a hutch filled with books ranging from suspense and sci-fi to nonfiction, while the master bedroom's large four-poster bed, with a luxurious black-and-gold damask comforter and pillows, was simply luxurious.

Peyton couldn't resist running her hands across the fabric; she couldn't wait to get under the sheets. "This is really nice."

Malik chuckled. "You'll love the feel of it on your skin." He was going to love having Peyton in his bed all night.

"I can't wait," Peyton said, smiling. "And the master bath?"

"Through the dressing area."

The large dressing area and walk-in closet led to a spectacular master bath. The same black granite countertops she'd seen in the kitchen were in the bathroom—a bathroom complete with above-the-counter sinks and wall-mounted faucets. The space screamed modern, with its travertine-tiled, separate shower stall and enormous sunken tub.

"You've created an oasis," Peyton commented, whirling around.

"One I can't wait to share with you," Malik replied.

Peyton visualized Malik's muscular body covered in

bubbles and she in the tub with him, and became heated just thinking about how much fun they'd have. "Are you ready to go?" she asked huskily, heading to the foyer. She'd hired a driver to take them to the show and to a late-night dinner afterwards.

"Indeed I am." Malik grabbed his keys off the console in the hallway and followed her out the door.

A short drive later, they were stepping out of the town car. Jude's show was located at an older theater, but Peyton didn't care. She was proud of her baby brother. When they arrived backstage, they were ushered to Jude's dressing room, which he shared with several other actors.

"Hey, kiddo." Jude beamed when Peyton handed him a bouquet of flowers. "What are these for?"

"For you, silly," Peyton replied. "We," she tucked her arm into Malik's, "wanted to say knock 'em dead. Or break a leg. Or whatever I'm supposed to say."

"So you're the mysterious man that has my sister so enraptured," Jude commented.

"That would be correct." Malik offered his hand. "Malik Williams."

Jude shook his hand. "Pleasure to meet you." Then Jude paused as he looked back and forth at Peyton and Malik. "You do realize your clothing matches? How annoyingly sweet, big sis."

Peyton swatted him on the arm. "Don't make fun."

"Don't shoot the messenger." Jude laughed. "Now, go." He pushed them towards the exit. "I have to get ready."

"All right." Peyton blew him a kiss. "We'll see you after the show."

They made their way to the auditorium, which was slowly starting to fill up. "I like Jude," Malik said, once they were seated. "He seems like a good kid."

"Kid? My brother's twenty-five."

"Yeah, but he has a real youthfulness about him. He's untouched by all the glamour that goes with the business," Malik said. "He's not jaded, much like his sister."

"What do you mean?"

Malik shrugged. "You're a very optimistic person, Peyton. You're always trying to change the world. That's what I love about you." Malik reached across and tucked some wayward strands of hair behind her ear.

A tiny knot formed in Peyton's stomach when Malik leaned over and kissed her. When the lights began to dim, signaling patrons to take their seats, they separated. As Malik leaned back into his chair and faced forward, one thing was clear, he couldn't wait for the night to be over so he could have Peyton all to himself.

After the two-hour show ended, Peyton and Malik waited for Jude to take him out for a celebratory dinner.

"Wasn't he fantastic? I just wish our parents were here to see him on opening night." Their mother had just had foot surgery a few weeks ago and was not permitted to travel. Peyton had tried unsuccessfully to convince them to make the drive, but her father had steadfastly refused. Either he flew or he didn't come. "Plus, I can't wait for them to meet you," Peyton gushed and squeezed his arm.

Malik didn't share in Peyton's excitement. His attachments usually ended before he met the parents. He was definitely in foreign territory.

Peyton glanced at Malik and saw his troubled expression. "Don't worry. They'll love you." Then she saw Jude and shrieked. She rushed towards him and planted a kiss on his cheek. "Ohmigod, you were fantastic!"

"Was I?" Jude asked. "I was so nervous. I almost flubbed my lines in that one scene."

"But you didn't. You were a hit."

"Let's hope the critics think so," Jude said. "I guess we'll know tomorrow."

"Until then, let's celebrate," Peyton said, grabbing Jude's hand. "Amber told me about this great place."

Jude glanced back at the staff huddled in a group. "Can we do it another time, sis? The gang's all going out clubbing."

"Oh," Peyton said, frowning. "I just wanted to celebrate with you." She was disappointed Jude wouldn't get to know Malik.

"And we will." Jude kissed her cheek, "Just not tonight. Malik, it was a pleasure meeting you." He shook Malik's hand. "And you—" he pointed to Peyton "—I'll call tomorrow. See ya."

Peyton watched Jude rush over and join the rest of the actors from the show and head towards the door.

"Well, I guess it's just the two of us," Malik observed, staring at Peyton. He pulled her closer to him. Although he knew Peyton wanted to celebrate Jude's debut, Malik was happy that they'd be alone for the duration of the evening.

Peyton looked up at Malik and found his eyes on her. They were smoldering with passion. "Yes, it is. I guess we'll have to find a way to while away the time."

"Hmm, I can think of a few things," Malik said, smiling broadly. "But why don't we get a bite to eat first, I'm starved." Food wasn't the only thing he was starving for, but it would suffice for the moment.

They ate at a fine dining establishment on Restaurant Row and enjoyed a wonderful Southern dinner, along with wine and conversation; but when the waitress asked if they wanted dessert, Malik and Peyton both glanced at each other. They wanted dessert, but of a different kind.

"No, thank you," Malik replied. He quickly settled the bill and they both could hardly contain their excitement as they waited for the driver outside the restaurant.

Once inside the car, Malik opened his arms. "Come here," he ordered.

Peyton's eyes melted into his and she quickly closed the distance between them, pressing her body against his. Malik eagerly brushed his lips back and forth over hers. His tongue was warm and moist and flirted with the corners of her mouth until her lips parted of their own volition. His tongue thrust deeply into her mouth in one long, arduous movement. He completely claimed her, as his tongue penetrated the innermost hollows of her mouth. They were so close, she could hear his heartbeat echoing her own.

"You have a very provocative mouth," Malik whispered in the stillness.

"So do you," Peyton said, nipping at his bottom lip. "And one that gives me immense pleasure." Peyton couldn't believe those words escaped her lips. She'd never been so blatantly wanton before. She just couldn't help herself with him.

"Does it?" Malik's eyes captured hers just as his fingertips rested against the top swell of her breasts. He was happy that Peyton felt comfortable speaking her mind and sharing how much she enjoyed him. They were making progress.

"Yes," Peyton whimpered against his ardent mouth as his tongue continued to plunge inside her mouth, while his hands shaped, molded and massaged her breasts.

When the car came to an abrupt stop, they both sat up startled. "I guess it's time we take this to the bedroom," Malik said, straightening both of their clothes.

"Oh yeah," Peyton said. When the driver came

around and opened her car door, she exited and followed Malik up the steps of his brownstone.

Once inside, Malik enfolded her in his arms. His breath was hot and quick as he said, "Let's go to bed."

Without turning on the lights, Peyton followed him, in a trancelike state, to his bedroom. They slowly removed each other's clothes, like they were peeling the layers of an onion, threw back the covers and joined each other in his four-poster bed.

Peyton's arms opened wide to receive Malik and accept his weight against her. She wanted to breathe him and absorb him until she was a part of him. With unhurried leisure, Malik kissed her. His lips warmly moved over hers again and again, his tongue probing the recesses of her mouth. Peyton's whole body came alive under the onslaught of his kisses, and she couldn't resist releasing a purr deep inside her.

Malik raised himself up on his shins and let his eyes feast on Peyton. They hungrily toured every inch of her body. When he finally dropped to the bed, he spread his hands over her derriere and drew Peyton's lower half to him. He kissed that silky nest with gentle fervency. A soft moan tore from Peyton's lips as his tongue and hands took liberties. Peyton enjoyed their quest, as he found and stroked that throbbing, intimate part of her that ached for a fulfillment that only he could provide.

He showered her face and temples with kisses. Peyton allowed her fingers to caress the rippled muscles of his chest, arms and back, and well-defined legs. Although he was lean, there was an inherent strength in Malik that totally turned her on. "You're so beautiful," Peyton murmured.

"So are you," Malik returned, laying atop her and parting her legs. When he guided himself into her center and pressed himself between the petals of her femininity, Peyton moaned his name and curled her arms around his neck to bring him closer.

As Peyton milked him, inviting him further and further into her body, Malik murmured, "Peyton, my love, slow down."

Peyton couldn't stop the tempo, her body writhed and undulated underneath him as Malik's face twisted with sublime pleasure. And when Peyton's body quickened uncontrollably, Malik finally let go of the reins and crested, as a bliss he'd never known took over him.

Chapter 10

"Malik." Richard shook his hand when he arrived at the center on Monday to go over the details of his contribution.

"Richard." Malik shook his hand. He was surprised to find that King had come alone, without any of his advisers. "Let's talk in my office." Malik led the way. "Please have a seat." Malik nodded to the small conference table.

"I have to admit I was surprised when Avery told me that you'd reconsidered," Richard said as he unbuttoned his suit jacket and sat down.

"Quite frankly, Richard, I realized what a disservice I would be doing to the center by turning down your offer. I can't make this personal. I have to do what's best for HCC."

"Well said." Richard was ready to let bygones be bygones if Malik was willing to move forward. "What do you have for me?"

Malik opened a manila folder and handed Richard a list. "My staff and I have compiled a list of the more pressing items that we would like to attend to first, and I've prepared a budget of the costs." Malik hoped Richard didn't get sticker shock at the final total.

"Updating the administrative offices is at the top of the list, I see," Richard commented, "and much needed." Richard glanced around at the peeling paint and worn carpet in Malik's office.

"I couldn't agree with you more. I've wanted this for a long time, which is why I already have schematic drawings." Malik pulled out the pages and handed them to Richard.

"You do?"

Richard sounded surprised that Malik was on top of things. "Yes, we hired an architect several months back when I proposed this idea to the CAN board, but we didn't get the green light. It's mostly painting and flooring. The main renovation is expanding the kitchen, which would require knocking down some walls and adding some cabinetry."

"This is excellent," Richard said as he perused the layout. "I'd like to fast-track this. I took the liberty of contacting a contractor whom I've used in the past, and I was going to suggest an architect—but I see you've already done your homework. My contractor may be able to get an early start permit while the drawings are being approved."

"How long do you think that'll take?"

"A couple of weeks."

"That quickly?"

"I know a few people. So everything should go smoothly, provided the drawings meet current building codes."

Malik grinned from ear to ear. "That's great."

"I'll set up a meeting with you and the contractor and you can discuss a schedule."

"You'd like to be a part of this?" Malik raised a brow. "I just assumed that you would pass this off to one of your subordinates."

"I came here alone, didn't I?" Richard asked. "You underestimate me, Malik. I gave my word to Avery, so I'm one-hundred-percent committed to this project." Richard popped open his suitcase and handed Malik an envelope.

"What's this?" Malik inquired.

"It's a check. It's small for now, but it'll allow you to get started right away ordering the necessary furniture, computer equipment and supplies, or whatever else you need. Once I review your budget, I'll deliver another check."

Malik was stunned and stared into Richard's green-eyed depths. It was then that Malik realized that maybe he'd been wrong about King. "Thank you." Malik shook his hand.

Richard rose and shook his head. "As long as you stay within this budget, you don't need to contact me about each penny you spend, Malik. Let's just plan on sitting down every couple of weeks and going over the numbers. If there's a problem, we'll tackle it then. Sound good?"

"Yes, that's fair." Malik was amazed at how reasonable Richard was being.

"I really must be going. I have another meeting to attend to." Richard buttoned his jacket.

"Thank you for *personally* stopping by."

"You're welcome," Richard replied, and left the room, leaving a stunned Malik in his wake.

Theresa walked in shortly afterwards and found Malik with a befuddled expression on his face.

Theresa glanced around the room. "It looks like the office is still intact," she teased. "So? What did Mr. King say about the budget?"

Malik shrugged. "Nothing." He couldn't understand it. "He basically gave me carte blanche to spend his money."

"I'm sure our budget is chump change in comparison to the deals he makes everyday."

"So true, so true." Malik jumped out of his seat and flew over to grab the older woman off her feet and swing her around. "We did it, Theresa! We did it!"

"Put me down," Theresa yelled and patted his hand. "Otherwise you're going to break your back."

"Oh, please." Malik set her to floor. "You're as light as a feather." Malik kissed her on the cheek. "And you know it."

Theresa blushed. "I haven't seen you this happy, this content, in a long time."

Malik turned and stared back at Theresa. She was right. He couldn't recall when he'd been this happy. Everything was going right in his life. His career was flourishing. He had a beautiful woman like Peyton Sawyer on his arm. Everything was right with the world.

"How's the situation with Kendra?" Amber asked Peyton after her last class.

"Not good."

"Why? What happened?"

"Well, I went over to her apartment to find out why she missed class and found her boyfriend had struck her. I was encouraging her to leave when he came home."

"Tell me you're joking?" Amber asked. "Peyton, I warned you that you were entering dangerous territory with this girl. And now look."

"Nothing happened."

"Nothing?" Amber asked, staring at Peyton. She was sure there was more to the story.

"Nothing." Peyton stated this more firmly, so her friend would believe her. "Her boyfriend told me to stay out of his affairs, but I can't do that, Amber. The girl needs help, which is why I convinced Malik to talk to her and give her some information."

"Do you think that helped?" Amber asked. She'd had a similar incident happen herself, in one of her women's studies classes. She'd see the girl come to class with a black eye, which her makeup had failed to disguise, or wearing a turtleneck in the middle of summer. When she tried to approach her, the girl had gotten angry and told her to mind her own business. Since then, Amber had resolved to stay out of students' affairs.

Peyton shook her head. "Can't say. I just hope that Kendra takes his advice."

"Did something else happen?" Amber wondered what Peyton wasn't saying.

"Yeah, sort of," Peyton replied. "Malik hinted that he would know about the sort of thing that Kendra's going through."

"Do you think there's something that Malik isn't telling you?"

"Maybe. He hasn't talked a lot about his past." Their conversation always touched upon her or their shared interests, but she knew nothing about where he came from. He'd only briefly mentioned that his mother had been a single mother before something bad happened. All she really knew was that the center had been like a second home for him and his friends. She just assumed that he'd meant as an afterschool hangout. But now she wondered if there wasn't more to the story.

"Don't make more of it than it really is. Sometimes it's hard for men to open up, and, you know, show vulnerability."

"I suppose you're right." Peyton's brow furrowed. "Maybe there's nothing to it." She resolved to bring up the subject with Malik again and this time she wasn't going to take no for an answer.

"Sage, sweetheart, where have you been?" Malik asked when she walked in with briefcase in tow to Dante's after work. He and Peyton were taking the night off so he could spend some quality time with his family. "It feels like I haven't seen you in ages."

When Malik kissed her cheek instead of pinching her nose, Sage knew something wasn't right. "What's going on?" she asked, looking back and forth at Quentin and Dante. "I know I've been busy on this big case, but I've never seen this one—" she pointed to Malik "—so happy. What happened to the brooding man I've come to know and love?"

"Replaced by a sappy guy in the throws of a committed relationship," Dante answered.

"No!" Sage said, and then took off the jacket that went with her pinstriped pants suit. "First playa—playa Quentin has a girlfriend and now Malik? What is the world coming to, Dante?" She turned to her best friend. "Are you starting to feel as left out as I am in this scenario?"

"C'mon, Sage, it's not like that," Malik said. "We're just dating. We're not a couple like Q and Avery."

"Have you not been seeing the woman at every possible occasion?" Quentin asked.

Malik thought about it. He had been seeing an awful lot of Peyton. They'd gone to a New York Knicks game, the Culture Fest in Battery Park and Caroline's Comedy

Club. But that was normal in the early dating stages. He didn't see anything unusual about it. Actually, the more time he spent in Peyton's company, the more he realized how truly fantastic she was. His desire for her had grown with each passing week; she was everything he wanted in a woman and more.

"Yes, but—"

"But nothing," Quentin interrupted him. "You're a couple."

"Well, maybe." He wasn't ready yet to swear off his bachelorhood. "But I am still the same Malik."

Sage peered at him. "Umm—no, I don't think so. Pretty soon the dreads and sexy five o'clock shadow will be gone and replaced with a sleek haircut and a clean jaw."

Malik laughed. "Never!" His dreads were a part of him. He'd been growing them for several years, and the thought of shearing them would be like shearing off a part of himself.

"You say that now," Sage teased, "but something tells me there are more changes to come."

"C'mon in." Malik waved Peyton in with some tongs when she arrived at his brownstone the following evening for dinner. "I was just grilling us some steaks outside on the terrace."

"I brought the wine." Peyton held up a bottle of red wine and leaned over to brush her lips across his.

"Hmm," Malik moaned. "Hold on to that thought. I have to check on the steaks."

Peyton followed him through the foyer and into the kitchen. When Malik went on the back deck, Peyton noticed he had the makings for a tossed salad assembled on the granite countertop. So she rolled up her sleeves and began cutting up the vegetables.

"What are you doing?" Malik asked when he came back inside. "I'm supposed to be making *you* dinner."

"I know," she said as she smiled, slicing the tomatoes. "I just thought I'd help you out. Is that a problem?" Peyton's eyes grew wide.

"Of course not," Malik replied. He took the knife out of her hand and pulled her into his arms. "Now, how about we pick up where we left off?" Malik's lips swept down on hers. He covered her mouth hungrily with his and his wet tongue dipped inside to taste her—and he wasn't disappointed. She tasted as sweet as honey.

"If you don't stop that," Peyton rasped, "Our steaks will be burned."

"Hmm," Malik moaned. "But you taste so much better than steaks." Malik nibbled on an earlobe.

Peyton pushed against his rock-hard chest. "How was work?"

"Work was fine," Malik said, trailing a path of wet kisses down her neck. "We're just waiting for the green light."

"Didn't you have a meeting with Richard?" Peyton inquired.

Malik lifted his head. "It went surprisingly well. Richard showed up alone, without his advisors, and we discussed the budget that I'd prepared."

"And?"

"And nothing," Malik said, shrugging. "He gave me a check and basically gave me carte blanche to do whatever was needed, provided I stay within budget."

"That's fantastic!" Peyton slapped his shoulder.

"Can you believe it?" His voice rose slightly. "He even has a contractor already lined up. The man sure didn't waste any time."

"See?" Peyton slapped his shoulder again. "I told

you everything was going to be fine. Is there anything I can do to help?"

"You can help Theresa select the paint, carpeting and tile. I'm color-blind when it comes to decorating. An interior decorator did my brownstone."

"I'd be happy to."

"I'd better go check on those steaks." Malik headed for the back door while Peyton put the finishing touch on their tossed salad by adding cucumbers and mushrooms. When she was finished, she mixed it and set it aside. She opened the oven and checked the potatoes. Satisfied they were ready, she took them out of the oven just as Malik returned, carrying a platter of rib-eye steaks.

"Mmm, those smell fantastic. What'd you put on them?"

"My secret rub recipe," Malik replied, placing the platter on the counter and opening the cabinet to take out two plates.

"Well, I might just have to pry it out of you," Peyton said, setting the potatoes on the plate. She doctored hers up by adding butter, cheese and sour cream from the fridge.

"I'm open to coercion." Malik grinned devilishly as he added a rib-eye to each plate.

When their plates were full, they brought them to the dining room table. "We can't forget the wine." Peyton rushed back into the kitchen. She returned carrying two generous glasses full and handed one to Malik. "I was thinking of surprising Jude by having my parents come for a visit to see his show now that mom's foot has healed."

"I'm sure he'd like that." Malik cut into his steak. "But I thought you said your parents hate to drive."

"They do. I thought I'd surprise them with some plane tickets."

"That's very generous of you," Malik replied. He'd never seen a caring family relationship with both parents before. Sure, he, Dante, Quentin and Sage had looked out for each other growing up, but they'd had to. Life at the orphanage where they all grew up was no joke. Malik had learned to develop a tough image, along with a bad temper.

It had originally been just the boys. Sage came into the fold after they'd found some bullies picking on her. She'd been short and scrawny and unable to defend herself. When they stepped in the bullying stopped, and so their foursome had been formed.

"I'm sure you would do the same for Quentin, Dante or Sage."

Malik nodded and took a forkful of salad.

"What about your biological family?" Peyton asked, digging into her baked potato. "You've never mentioned them or how you came to meet your friends."

Malik sighed. He'd wondered when Peyton would inquire about his family. He'd made a point of avoiding it during their conversations, so he was sure Peyton's curiosity was piqued. "My mother died when I was young." More like abandoned him, but he left out that part.

"And your father?"

"Never knew him."

Peyton sighed. She was frustrated by Malik's brief remarks. Why did she have to pry information out of him? What was he hiding? "And? How did you meet your friends?"

"At an orphanage," Malik replied. "We all bonded because of our mutual misfortune and vowed to stick together. And we did."

Peyton clutched his hand. "Malik, I had no idea. I'm so sorry. How long were you there?"

"From the time I was ten years old until I was eighteen and considered a legal adult. After that—" Malik bunched his shoulders "—we all moved out and got a place together."

Peyton digested the information. His mother had died so young and left him alone at such a tender age. It was incredible that Malik and his friends hadn't become a statistic. They'd all persevered and become successful in their respective careers. "So, the center—"

"Was a place of refuge," Malik finished. "We went there when we needed to get away from the orphanage. We'd do our homework, shoot hoops, or whatever else, to avoid going back to our jail. If it wasn't for Andrew…"

"Your mentor?"

Malik nodded. "Who knows where I would have ended up? You see, I had a humongous chip on my shoulder back then, and the only person who saw through all that bravado was Andrew."

Peyton nodded. Now it all made sense. The center had been like a second home to him. No wonder he'd been so resistant to Richard, someone he'd seen as a threat to the center. "I see why you respect him so much."

"I do."

"Thank you for sharing your story with me." She was encouraged that Malik had revealed his past to her. "How about I clear up these dishes?" Peyton kissed him on the cheek and took the empty plates back to the kitchen.

As she walked away, Malik felt like a heel. He'd let Peyton assume that his mother had died, leaving him an orphan. The truth of the matter was that although the courts had removed Malik from his mother's custody due to child abuse, Joe had never been arrested, because his mother had refused to testify against him. What he'd said was dishonest, but he just wasn't ready yet to share that part of himself with Peyton. Malik doubted if he would ever be ready.

Chapter 11

"Hey, Mom, guess who?" Peyton said from her apartment on Thursday. She had no classes and was kicking off her heels and taking a break from lecturing, researching and volunteering, to just relax.

"Peyton, darling, it's so good to hear your voice," her mother, Lydia Allen, said from the other end, in Cleveland. "How's New York treating my sweetheart?"

"Great!" Peyton replied. "Actually, better than that."

"Really? How so?"

"I love my new teaching gig at NYU, Mom. I have a great group of students that aren't afraid of getting their hands dirty and volunteering."

"Sounds good, but why do I have a feeling there's a 'but' in there?"

"There's one student, Kendra, a single mother who's in a domestic violence situation…"

"Have you given her information on organizations that can help her?"

"Yes. Malik and I both have, but—"

Her mother interrupted her. "There are no 'buts.' You've done all you can do. The choice is up to her. You can't force someone to get help."

"I know that in my head, but in my heart I feel so utterly helpless."

"You know you've always had a savior complex." Her mother chuckled.

"What do you mean?"

"Even when you were a child, you'd want to take in every stray cat and dog. Remember when you were eight and you wanted to take in a bird whose wings were clipped? You nursed that poor bird back to health, and when it finally found the strength to fly away you were utterly devastated."

Peyton nodded. "I remember that. I was so heartbroken. I cried for days."

"You can't save everyone," her mother replied. "You can only do what you can with the tools you have. Now that we've tackled that subject. Why don't you tell me who this Malik person is? And why am I just now hearing about him?"

"Oh, Mother, he's great." Peyton sighed and fell back against the sofa. "His name is Malik Williams. He's the director at the community center where I'm volunteering. He's compassionate and giving and totally gorgeous." It amazed her that just like with David, she'd fallen hard and fast and there was no looking back.

"Sounds like you really fancy him?" Lydia asked happily.

"I do. We share the same interests and value system. We believe in family and in helping others. Can you believe it, Mom? I finally found someone who is as philanthropic as we are."

"He sounds too good to be true."

"You have to meet him," Peyton stated.

"Do you really think that's wise? You've only been in New York a short time," her mother commented. "You don't want to scare the poor man off by meeting the parents too soon, do you?"

"Of course not. But you guys have to come, because how else are you going to see Jude's new show?"

"You have a point there." Lydia had heard nothing but great things from Peyton and the New York newspapers that Jude had e-mailed her.

"It's settled then," Peyton replied. "I bought two round-trip tickets from Cleveland to New York for you for next week. You'll come and see Jude's show and meet Malik."

"Thank you, dear, you really are a wonderful daughter."

"And you're an even better mother," Peyton said. "Tell Dad I said hello." Peyton was excited when she hung up. She couldn't wait for Malik to meet her parents.

Malik had just returned from making a special trip over to the Brooklyn center and treating the entire staff to pizza and sodas so they wouldn't feel neglected, when Loretta buzzed his intercom. "Malik, you have a visitor."

Malik anticipated it might be Logan Hayes, his contractor. He suspected that they'd received their early start permit and be able to start demolition in the kitchen as early as next week. The contractor was sure he wouldn't have a problem getting the drawings approved. "Send him in," Malik said.

Malik glanced up and, instead of seeing Logan, he found Joe Johnson at his doorway. "What are *you* doing here?"

"I came to see if you had a change of heart," Joe said, barging into his office. "It doesn't look like anything has changed since the last time I was here, so you're probably pretty desperate right now and ready to negotiate." Joe smirked.

Malik rose to his feet. "Sorry to disappoint you, Joe, but I'm far from desperate. The center has a sponsor. A multimillion-dollar-conglomerate backing the renovations."

Joe's smirk quickly turned into a frown. "Who would be dumb enough to donate money to this shack?"

"Richard King," Malik replied smoothly.

"The business mogul?"

"The same," Malik said, smiling. "So, as you can see, we will not need Johnson Construction's services—not now or in the future."

"Oh, you think you're a big shot now, huh," Joe replied, walking towards Malik, "just because you conned King into giving you some money. King probably feels sorry for you."

Malik paused to gather patience. "That's far from the truth. Unlike you, Joe, some people do things out of the goodness of their hearts."

"Oh, please, I'm sure you laid it on thick. Poor, pathetic Malik grew up as an orphan. When you and I both know the truth, which is that your mother didn't want you because you were a worthless little punk."

Malik took a threatening step towards him. "I've had just about enough of you. Get out!" Malik pointed to the door.

"Am I getting to you, Mr. Director," Joe taunted. "Surely, nothing can get under your skin."

Malik reached out and grabbed Joe by the collar. He wanted to beat the crap out of him, but instead he counted to ten and shoved him backward. "You get out of here before I call the police and have you escorted out."

Joe straightened his back and brushed off his collar as if Malik weren't good enough to touch him. "You came from nothing and you will always be nothing, Malik Williams."

Joe's words lingered long after he'd left, causing Malik to slam his fist on the desk.

Peyton was determined to speak with Kendra after her lecture on Friday. She'd given the young mother a wide berth in the hopes that she would take Malik's advice, but Kendra had said nothing.

As soon as class was over, Kendra darted out of the room. Peyton grabbed her satchel and flew off down the hall behind her. When she exited, Peyton found Omar and Kendra arguing in front of the building.

"Get in the car!" Omar grabbed Kendra by the arm.

"No!" Kendra jerked her arm away. "I told you we're staying at my grandmother's until you get some help to deal with your anger issues."

"You are not taking my daughter away," Omar replied, "so get in." Omar pushed Kendra towards the passenger door.

"What do you think you're doing?" Peyton called out, running down the stairs. "Get your hands off of her."

Omar whirled around. "The lady professor again." Omar shook his head. "Don't you ever learn? I told you to mind your own business. This is between Kendra and me."

Peyton reached inside her handbag for her cell phone. "Either you take your hands off her right now, or I'm calling campus security." Peyton held up her cell.

Omar stepped away from Kendra and walked around

to the driver's door. "I don't need that kind of hassle," he said and jumped into his Mustang. Once inside, he turned on the engine and rolled down the passenger window. "Know this, Kendra," he yelled, "it's not over." Seconds later, he was speeding away.

"Are you okay?" Peyton asked, touching Kendra's arm.

Kendra nodded and rubbed her arm. "I'm fine. Just a little shaken."

"If you like, we can talk in my office," Peyton suggested.

"You don't mind?"

"C'mon." Peyton wrapped her arm around Kendra's shoulder. "My office is a couple of blocks away."

They walked a short distance to her office and climbed the stairs to the second floor. Peyton unlocked the door and switched on the light. Kendra followed her inside and sat down.

"Why don't I make you some tea?" Peyton suggested, and plugged in a hot water kettle that she kept on hand for stressful occasions. She pulled two mugs and a box of herbal tea out of her drawer and placed two bags inside. "So, when did you move out?"

"When Omar was at work one night, I packed up a few things and left. After reading those horror stories in the pamphlets that Malik gave me, I realized I didn't want me and my daughter to be another statistic. And that, as much as I love Omar, he needs some help. He's only hit me once or twice, but he's manhandled me lots of times. And if I let this continue it's going to escalate and I could wind up in the hospital."

"What you did took bravery and courage, and I'm really proud of you," Peyton replied.

"Thanks, Dr. Sawyer. You've really been amazing,"

Kendra said. "I would have never found the courage to leave Omar on my own."

"Don't give me props just yet. I want to get you the help you need."

"You think I might be able to meet with Mr. Williams again?" Kendra asked, "I have those forms filled out."

"Of course. Mr. Williams has an open-door policy," Peyton replied. She felt strangely odd, being so formal about Malik. When the tea kettle whistled, Peyton poured steaming water into the two mugs. "I'm sure he'll be very happy to see you. And if you'd like, I can come with you. I'm done with classes."

Kendra smiled. "I would like that."

After they finished their tea, they hopped a train to Harlem and walked to the center.

"Hey, Loretta," Peyton said when they walked through the reception doors. "Is Malik in?"

Loretta smiled. "For you, he certainly is. Go on in."

"C'mon, Kendra," Peyton said, pushing through the double doors.

Malik's door was open, as always. "Hey there!"

When he looked up from his computer and saw Peyton, Malik smiled. Peyton was just what he needed after Joe Johnson's visit.

"Hey, gorgeous." Malik rose from his desk and walked towards Peyton, but she halted him with her hand.

"I didn't come alone," she said, and Kendra peeked from the other side of the door.

"Kendra! I'm so glad you came. Come on in." Malik winked at Peyton and waved them inside. "Please have a seat."

"I filled out all those forms." Kendra reached inside her knapsack and produced the folder Malik had given her.

"Great. We have a volunteer that can look it over for you and make sure there are no problems. Then she'll file it for you. It typically takes as little as four but up to eight weeks to actually see funds."

"But…"

"I know what you're thinking. How are you going to get by in the interim? We get a lot of job postings here, and they are posted in our computer tech room if you'd like to peruse them."

"I think I'll do that," Kendra said and abruptly left the room.

"Hmm, now that I have you all to myself…" Malik pulled Peyton out of her seat and onto his lap.

"Malik, the door is wide open." Peyton glanced at the door. "What if someone sees?"

"Peyton, I'm sorry to have to be the one to tell you this—" Malik grinned "—but everyone already knows about us. This is a small office, you know."

Peyton colored. "Are we that obvious?"

"Apparently so."

"Are you okay?" she asked. Tension was etched across his face.

"It's been a hellacious week here," Malik said. He couldn't tell her the real reason behind his unrest, which was that he'd come face-to-face with his past again, and it had made him see red.

"I understand," Peyton said. "Why don't you come over to my place and I can help you relax?"

Malik sighed. "That's sounds great."

"I'll see you later." Peyton leaned down and gave him a searing kiss before leaving his office. When he came by her apartment, Peyton intended to give him a night he'd never forget.

* * *

Peyton stood in front of the full-length mirror in a satin flyaway baby doll with matching bikini panties she'd purchased from Victoria's Secret, staring at the sultry image reflecting back. She'd never worn any of their sexy ensembles before, even though she'd always wanted one. She'd been content to sleep in one of David's old T-shirts. Malik would be surprised when she opened the door in this hot number, Peyton knew as she slipped on the matching satin robe.

Earlier, she'd sensed that something was bothering Malik, though he put on a good show when she stopped by the community center earlier. She couldn't put her finger on what it was, so she'd determined to cure him of his funk with a little TLC.

Walking over to her entertainment center, she turned on some KEM and his jazzy music filled the air. Several strategically placed candles were lit for ambience. Now all she had to do was wait.

Peyton nearly jumped out of her skin when a loud knock sounded on the door. It was time. Let the seduction begin. Through the peephole she saw that it was her man, and threw open the door just as she undid the sash on her robe.

"Wow!" Malik gasped. "Is this for me?"

"Sure is." Peyton pulled him inside and shut the door.

Malik fell back against it and got an eyeful of Peyton's seductive figure in the sexy getup. He loved seeing her long legs and gorgeously taut thighs that would be wrapped around him before long. "Come here," he growled.

Peyton rushed over and he claimed her lips, crushing her to him. His kiss, slow and thoughtful, sent spirals of ecstasy flowing right through Peyton. As his kisses deepened, Peyton relaxed and sunk into his cushioning embrace, and before she knew it they were sliding down the door. Malik's hands gripped her body and brought her into full contact with his burgeoning erection. Peyton's nipples grew taut beneath the thin fabric and she ground herself against him.

"We'd better take this to the bedroom," Malik rasped and jumped to his feet. Otherwise he'd be taking her right there, in the middle of her hallway.

Peyton nodded and took his hand as he helped her off the floor. Blood was coursing through her veins like a river and she couldn't deny the aching need. She wanted Malik inside her.

They walked to her bedroom, and once there Peyton helped relieve Malik of his clothing. He was wearing much too much. Once he was naked, they came together on top of the softness of her bed, but that was the only thing that was soft. Malik's erection was hard and jutted out, waiting for her, and Peyton couldn't wait to ride it. She blushed at the thought. She was freer and more liberated in the bedroom than she'd ever been.

She titled her head and he lowered his. Their lips met and they brushed them softly against each other. Her tongue slid across his lips and he opened his mouth allowing her entry. His hands roamed over her entire body, and everywhere he touched her, she burned. Peyton liked the feeling and she wanted more, more of Malik.

She eased down the straps of her flyaway baby doll and heard crackle from the candle's flame seconds before Malik rolled her to the side and took one of her nipples firmly in his mouth. A jolt went straight through Peyton and she entwined her fingers in his dreads, holding him to her breast. Malik knew what she wanted and sucked harder and faster, and when he was done with one nipple he shifted to the other breast and feasted. Meanwhile he reached down and slid her bikini panties down her legs and flung them away as if they were nothing more than an inconvenience. Then he slid his finger inside the slick folds of her feminine center. Peyton was already wet and ready for him. As he slowly slid his finger in and out, Peyton's pulse quickened and she gyrated, eager for release. But it wasn't time yet. He was going to make her wait.

Then Malik proceeded to kiss and nibble every square inch of Peyton's body, starting from the nape of her neck, down to her aching breasts and her taut stomach, before finally coming to the tender flesh of her inner thighs. As he hovered over the swollen lips of her sex, Peyton's eyes were firmly shut and Malik could swear she was holding her breath when he dipped inside to taste her. He tongued her feverishly and she involuntarily jerked forward.

"Easy, love. Just enjoy it." Malik spread her legs farther apart and flicked his tongue over that highly intimate part of her. At the same time, he sank a finger inside her and moved it slowly in and out.

"Oh, Malik!" Peyton moaned.

"Yes, baby." Malik didn't stop, but continued gliding his finger in and out while he tongued her until she shuddered. Then he quickly sat up and tore open a shiny foil package from her nightstand drawer and protected them both in a flurry of motion.

But Peyton refused to let him take over. It was her turn. She pushed him down on the bed, straddled his lap and took him deep inside her body. So deep, she wasn't sure where he ended and she began. He filled every part of her. It sounded like a cliché, she knew, but it was true. She loved feeling the tight sinew of his muscles as she gripped him, hearing the sounds of their lovemaking mixed with the music, and smelling the cologne on his sweaty, sculpted body. He felt so good and so right. This wasn't just an act of passion for Peyton anymore, it was an act of love.

When Malik lifted her Peyton wanted to cry out and protest, but then he lowered her back over his shaft again and again, deeper and deeper, until pressure built deep within her and an onslaught of emotions assaulted her. "Oh, yes," she hissed. Only Malik could build the tension, slow and rhythmic at first, to a fever pitch until she exploded in a million pieces. When Peyton wiggled her bottom one more time, she heard him cry out his own release.

Afterward a glow spread through Peyton's entire body. Only Malik could make her feel that kind of passion, and as she lay on top of him and drifted off to sleep, Peyton admitted to herself that what she felt for Malik was love. In a short time she'd fallen head over heels with his kindness, with his strength and with his passion. She couldn't believe it had happened so quickly. After David, she'd thought she would never find that kind of love again. She'd closed off her heart to the idea, but somehow Malik found his way inside.

Loving Malik didn't mean that she didn't love David or that he would somehow replace him. She would always love David. He was her childhood sweetheart and first love, but Malik was her future.

Malik too, had fallen asleep, but his dreams were far from blissful. He tossed and turned. Images of Joe using an extension cord to beat him because he didn't take out the trash or because he got a C in school, or because he was just plain drunk, flashed through Malik's dreams. He could see his mother, Vanessa, cowering in the corner, afraid to speak or move for fear he'd backhand her. Malik yelled out to her for help, but she wouldn't help him. "Mommy, help me. Mommy, help me."

In the distance, he could hear someone calling out to him. "Malik, Malik." But all he could do was hold up his hands to try to fend off Joe's blows. Remembering the sting as Joe hit him and the welts that formed afterwards caused Malik to finally awaken and sit straight up.

"Malik, honey." Peyton was beside him, stroking back his dreads. "It's okay. It was just a bad dream."

Malik turned and swept Peyton in his arms. He held her so tightly, Peyton could hardly breathe.

"Malik, it's okay. I'm not going anywhere."

He grasped her face in his hands and stared at her for several long seconds as if he didn't recognize her. "I'm sorry." Malik slowly released her. He'd gotten caught up in the past.

"That must have been some dream," Peyton commented, "to cause you to break out in a cold sweat." She'd never seen him like this. His back was bathed in sweat and his breathing was labored. "Let me get you a towel." Peyton slipped out of bed and returned with a damp hand towel. She dabbed at his brow and his back. She didn't know what the dream was about, but it had clearly shaken him.

"Thank you."

Peyton smiled. "You're welcome." She'd do anything for him, because in a short time she'd fallen head over heels for him. "Do you want to talk about it?"

Malik shook his head.

"Are you sure? Talking about it helps. And I'm here to listen." Peyton desperately wanted Malik to feel like he could confide in her and tell her anything. When he didn't answer, she continued. "I think you may have called out for your mother."

"I doubt that, but I'm fine, really." Malik patted her knee, effectively dismissing her concerns. "Plus, I don't remember it anyway."

Peyton doubted that was true. He remembered. He just didn't want to share it with her. She didn't want to press, so she pulled him into her arms. Malik laid his head down between her breasts and Peyton held him there close to her heart for the rest of the night.

Chapter 12

On Monday, Peyton was in a foul mood. When she woke up on Saturday, she'd found Malik had gone. She didn't even get a goodbye kiss. Nothing. He'd shown vulnerability and it must have scared him because he'd high-tailed it out of there as quick as he could and hadn't called her for the rest of the weekend, either.

There was more to Malik's past than he could say to her. In his nightmare, he'd called out to his mother and he'd had his arms up as if he were defending himself. Was it that bad growing up in the orphanage? Did he have to defend himself from bullies?

Peyton met Amber for lunch to ask her advice. When she arrived at the French bistro, Amber was already there. The hostess showed Peyton to the table and she leaned down to give Amber a quick hug.

"Hey, you," Amber said. "When you called and said

we had to meet, I knew something was up. Is it Malik? Kendra? Or both?"

"Why would you automatically assume it has something to do with either of them?" Peyton asked.

"Because you've been a tad preoccupied," Amber replied. "Have you even had time to work on publishing any articles?"

"For your information, I have two articles in the works that I'm going to submit to several educational journals."

Amber smiled. "Good. I'm glad to hear you haven't completely abandoned your career for a man or to play do-gooder."

"Ouch." Peyton frowned. "Should I get up and come back in? You're not usually so sharp."

"I'm sorry, girlfriend," Amber apologized. "I just went on a horrible date with this cheapo last night, who wanted to split the bill fifty-fifty when *he* asked me out. Can you believe the nerve?"

"I can," Peyton said. Which is why she was so happy that she'd found Malik. Dating was like gambling. Sometimes you win and sometimes you'd lose.

"So, why'd you want to meet?"

"It's Malik."

"I knew it." Amber snickered.

Peyton rolled her eyes. "He had a terrible nightmare the other night and woke up in a cold sweat."

"Is that all?"

Peyton shook her head. "That's the problem. I think it was more than just a bad dream. He was calling out for his mother. And according to him, she died when he was young, which is why he ended up in an orphanage."

"So, maybe he was having nightmares about losing her so early in life, or growing up in an orphanage. I can't imagine that was easy."

"Perhaps," Peyton responded. "Or perhaps he's keeping something from me. He was genuinely frightened and wouldn't let me go the rest of the night. But when I woke up the next morning, he was gone. Poof!" She snapped her fingers. "And he hasn't called me since."

"Maybe he's embarrassed. You know how men are. They don't want us to see them as weak."

"I know that's part of it, but I'm just having a nagging feeling that something's going on," Peyton explained. "I just wish he'd let me in."

At the concern and care in Peyton's voice, Amber stared deeply into her eyes. "You're in love with him, aren't you?"

Peyton inhaled. If she couldn't admit it to her best friend, who could she admit it to? "I am."

"Oh, Peyton," Amber sighed, "don't you think it's too soon?"

"It's been five years since I lost David," Peyton replied. "No, I don't think it's too soon. Malik's a wonderful man."

"Who, as you said yourself, is clearly tortured. I hope he's worth it."

Peyton couldn't believe what she was hearing. "Of course he's worth it. C'mon, Amber, it's not like I haven't been in love before. I'm not a novice, I mean, sure I was when it came to sex, but that was different I'd only had one lover. I know what love is because I've had true love before."

"And because you have, maybe you're desperate to have that feeling again," Amber answered cynically.

Peyton shook her head. "This is more than infatuation, Amber. But listen, I understand what you're saying, okay? And I'm not rushing into this. I haven't even told Malik how I feel. For the moment, I'm keeping it to

myself until I'm sure the feelings are reciprocated."
Peyton didn't want to put her feelings on the line yet
because she wasn't sure of Malik's feelings for her.

"Good idea."

"Now can we eat, please?"

"Sure can," Amber replied and they ordered their lunch.

"Theresa, what's all this?" Malik asked when he came
into the office later that morning, after stopping by the
Brooklyn center to check on a problem with the heating
system, and found Theresa and Denise Burke in his office.

"The contractor dropped off some carpet, tile and
paint samples and since they've already completed the
demo on the conference room floor, I opened up your
office. I hope you don't mind?" Theresa replied.

Malik shook his head as he took off his leather
bomber jacket and placed it on the hook behind his door.
"Of course not. Is there any coffee?" he asked, rubbing
his hands together. The weather was already changing
and becoming cooler. It was definitely feeling like fall.

"Sure, there's some in the kitchen."

Malik left and returned several minutes later sipping
a steaming cup.

"What do you think of this?" Denise held a paint
swatch against a carpet sample.

Malik nodded. "Hmm, looks fine to me." Malik went
over to his desk and checked his voice mail. There was
a message from Peyton.

Malik felt guilty for running out on her the way he
did on the weekend, but he just wasn't in the mood for
more questions. Seeing Joe had rustled up some demons
he thought were long since buried. He hadn't been
prepared for them to rise back to the surface. It didn't
help that he suspected Peyton knew that there was more

than he was letting on. He couldn't tell her about the abuse he'd suffered as a child. He liked the way she looked at him as though he were a hero. Malik didn't want that to ever change.

He deleted her message without calling her back and turned on his computer to get to work. He ignored the two women as they haggled over colors. When they had compiled several options, Denise left, but Theresa stayed behind.

"Is everything all right?" she asked. Malik wasn't acting like himself. He was oddly quiet and much more reserved.

"Everything's fine," Malik replied, typing an e-mail.

"And Peyton?" Theresa inquired.

"We're good."

"Then your mood must have something to do with your being at odds with Andrew," Theresa deduced. When Malik glanced up at her, Theresa knew she'd hit her mark. "You should talk to him, Malik." Theresa came forward and sat in front of him.

"It won't change anything."

"But it might make you feel better. I know you don't like being on the outs with him."

Theresa was right about that. It had certainly stuck in his craw that they hadn't seen eye-to-eye on Joe. They'd rarely spoken since their disagreement. Malik would love to be able to talk to Andrew. "And you know why."

"I do, and I can't much blame you," Theresa said. "But don't let a difference of opinion come between the bond that you and Andrew share. Joe Johnson isn't worth it. Promise me you will fix this rift."

"I will." Malik crossed his heart. That's why he adored Theresa. She took no prisoners.

"All right, well my job here is done," she said and left the room.

* * *

Peyton arrived to the center later that evening for her weekly Sister-to-Sister session with the young African-American and Latin women in the community. She was a little early because she was hoping to catch Malik before he left, but when she got to his office it was already locked. When did Malik Williams, workaholic that he was, actually leave on time? And was he avoiding her?

Bummed, Peyton proceeded to the lounge, but caught Theresa on her way out. She was putting on her coat and locking up her office when Peyton came forward.

"Peyton, how are you?" Theresa kissed her cheek.

"I'm good," Peyton replied. "I was just on my way to my Sister-to-Sister meeting."

"You're doing such a great job with those girls," Theresa said. "Several mothers have praised your efforts."

"Thank you, Theresa. That's so great to hear."

Theresa glanced at Malik's door. "I take it you were looking for Malik?"

"Oh, yes. I thought I'd say hello before the meeting, but it looks like I've missed him."

"He said he needed to leave early to take care of some personal business. It's a shame you weren't here earlier, you could have seen some of the paint and carpet samples we picked out."

"Samples?" Peyton was crushed. She'd thought Malik wanted her help with decorating. She was sure Malik had asked for her assistance. Hadn't he said he was color-blind?

"Our contractor had some great selections for us to choose from," Theresa gushed. "Just wait until this place is done. It's going to be a whole new center. Well, I got to go. I'll talk to you soon."

Theresa rushed down the hall, leaving Peyton with the distinct feeling that Malik was giving her the cold shoulder.

After a short train ride, Malik arrived at Dante's. Dante was seating several customers when he came in. "Hey, Malik," Dante said, smiling, "you have someone waiting for you." Dante nodded in the direction of one of the booths where Andrew sat waiting.

"Thanks, Dante." Malik patted him on the back and walked towards the booth and slid in.

Andrew nodded. "Neutral territory, huh?"

"I thought it was best," Malik said. Dante's was a safe haven for him.

"Malik," Andrew began, "I'm sorry—"

But Malik interrupted him. "I'm sorry too." He never meant any disrespect to Andrew. He held his mentor in high regard. There was no one he respected more, except maybe Quentin and Dante.

"I'm sorry if you felt I undermined your authority," Andrew said. "That really wasn't my intention. I know what Joe Johnson did to you and your mother, and you have every right not to want to accept money from the man. I guess sometimes I get on my moral high horse."

"Sometimes," Malik answered.

"So we're friends again?" Andrew extended his hand.

Malik shook his hand. "We never stopped being friends. As a matter of fact, I've needed to talk to someone."

"Really? What about?"

"Joe. Peyton. Everything." Malik sighed and lowered his head. He paused. He had to talk to someone. "I… I've been having those nightmares again."

"Like when you were younger?"

Malik nodded. "Seeing Joe again has brought all

those old fears and memories bubbling to the surface. And the sad part about it is that I'd like to talk to Peyton, but I can't. She grew up in a loving home, surrounded by a family that loved her."

"Why not tell her?" Andrew asked. "I'm sure she'd understand."

"Because she'd see me as less of a man," Malik answered honestly. "How can I admit to being abused? How can I admit that my stepfather used me as a punching bag and not become less in her eyes?"

"Malik, you couldn't control what happened to you. You were a child."

"I know, I know. But this is different. Peyton is an amazing woman. She's smart and beautiful and sexy and kind. She deserves a man that can open up himself to her completely, and I'm just not sure that I can do that. I'm damaged goods." He had so many psychological issues to deal with—much more than the average man she'd encounter.

"That's not true, Malik. You have a lot to offer," Andrew replied, "and I think you're selling Peyton short if you don't confide in her. Tell her what happened. Didn't you just say that's she's kind and understanding?"

"She is."

"You and I both have seen her volunteer. She gives of herself so freely to others. What makes you think you'd be any different?"

"I don't know." Malik shrugged. Maybe deep down he thought he wasn't worthy of having a woman like Peyton Sawyer. Maybe on a deeper level, Joe Johnson's claims that Malik would never be anything, never amount to anything, never be worth anything, caused the words to sink in.

"Trust me, I'm right." Andrew smiled. "You'll see."

* * *

After her meeting was over, Peyton called Malik on his cell phone and this time he answered. "Hey, stranger," Peyton said, trying to sound nonchalant.

"Hey, baby," Malik replied.

"Are you at home?" Peyton queried. "I was leaving the center and thought, since I was in neighborhood, I'd stop by."

"No, I'm not, but I'll be there in about five minutes." Malik was just exiting the subway station and walking down the block to his brownstone.

"All right, I'll see you in a few." Peyton hung up. She said goodbye to the security guard and headed out the door. She just hoped that when she arrived things would be back to normal between the two of them.

Malik opened a bottle of wine. The wine was to help him relax so he'd appear mellow by the time Peyton arrived. He wasn't nearly there yet, when she rang his doorbell. When he opened the door he found Peyton smiling.

"Hi." Peyton came inside and started removing her wool jacket. Although she was angry with him, even in jeans and a cashmere sweater he could still stir her senses.

"Here, let me help you with that." Malik eased the coat off her shoulders with one hand while holding the wine goblet in the other.

"Do you have another one of those?" Peyton asked. It had been a long day and she could sure use a glass.

"I sure do," Malik said, "but first…" He circled his arms around her waist and pulled her to him. He dipped his head and pressed his lips to hers.

When they parted, Peyton sensed Malik was putting forth a good effort to appear like all was normal, so she played along. She followed him down the hall to the kitchen, where he took a bottle of white wine out of the fridge and poured her a glass. "Here you are, my dear."

Peyton accepted the wine and drank deeply. She hopped onto a bar stool at the breakfast nook and stared at Malik. He obviously wasn't going to address the fact that he'd left Saturday morning without saying goodbye, nor returned any of her calls. "I told you my parents were coming, right?"

"Oh, yeah," Malik said, leaning against the stove. "I remember you mentioning it." He wasn't ready to meet her parents yet, but Peyton was so excited he didn't have the heart to tell her no.

"They'll be staying in my guest room," Peyton said. "So unfortunately, there won't be any sleepovers while they're here."

"I understand." Malik nodded. "I would never disrespect you in front of your parents."

"Oh, okay." Peyton laughed derisively and sipped her wine. "I'm glad to see you won't miss me."

"Of course I'll miss you." Malik walked over to the bar and stood between her legs. "I'm just honoring your request."

"Right," Peyton said, nodding. He was probably looking forward to some distance.

"C'mon, let's go listen to some jazz." Malik pulled her off the stool and towards the living room. "I got this great CD from this guy off the street."

Peyton laughed. Malik was always supporting the underdog. She just wished he showed the same support to their relationship.

They spent the remainder of the evening lounging on the couch before retiring to bed. She would have to get up and run home and change in the morning before her afternoon class. She'd just wanted to try to connect with Malik and see if he'd open up.

After brushing her teeth with the spare toothbrush she kept as his apartment, and washing her face, Peyton climbed into bed wearing one of Malik's old T-shirts. He held open the covers so she could slide in under the cool sheets next to his warm body. Her bottom nestled comfortably against his groin, but despite how good it felt, Peyton was still bothered by Malik's odd behavior and decided to confront him.

She turned over and Malik's dark brown eyes focused on hers in the shadows. "Why did you leave so early on Saturday without saying goodbye?"

"I had a lot of errands to run."

Plausible excuse. "You didn't return my calls today."

"It was busy at the center. It was one crisis after another. Are you upset with me?" Tension ebbed and flowed off Peyton's entire body.

"Yes, I am," Peyton said, leaning over and turning on the nightstand lamp. "You ignored me. I don't appreciate it."

"I'm sorry, Peyton. I had a long day. Can't we just go to sleep?" Malik asked.

"No, we can't." Peyton didn't like his exasperated tone, and she sat upright. Malik followed suit. "Because there's more to it than that. There's something you're not telling me."

"There's nothing going on."

"Good heavens, Malik!" Peyton jumped off the bed and spun around to face him. "You're lying. Why do you continue to leave me in the dark? Why won't you let me in? Why won't you let me into your life?"

Tears welled up in Peyton's eyes. "If you're having a bad day I want to know about it. If something or someone has upset, you can talk to me. I want to help make it right for you. Don't you know that you don't have to go through life alone anymore? I'm here for you, and not just with my body."

Malik hung his head low. "I'm sorry, Peyton. I'm trying. I've never been in a relationship before, so this is all new to me."

Peyton came over to his side of the bed and kneeled in front of him. "At some point, you have to take a risk. Don't you think it's time for you to finally let someone inside here?" She pointed to his heart.

Malik shrugged and Peyton could see the wall around his heart shutting her out. "Maybe you want more than I can give."

Peyton sighed. "Fine, then I'm going to go home." Peyton rose to her feet. She loved him, but she wasn't sure he was capable of reciprocating that love, and it broke her heart.

"What are you talking about?" Malik said with some panic. "It's late. Come back to bed, Peyton."

Peyton shook her head. She would like nothing better than to fall asleep with Malik's arms wrapped around her—but at what cost? She had her own heart to look out for. "Not tonight." She went to the adjoining bathroom and shut the door behind her. She turned on the running water to block out the sound of her crying.

Peyton emerged fully dressed fifteen minutes later and found Malik sitting on the edge of the bed, having another glass of wine. "I called a cab," he said.

"Thanks." Peyton headed to the foyer to gather her belongings. She was putting on her coat when she heard Malik walking up behind her barefoot, and she spun around.

"Peyton, I think you're an incredibly smart, sexy woman."

"Why do I have a feeling there's a 'but' coming in there somewhere?" Peyton asked, folding her arms across her chest.

Malik sighed. "I think we need to take a break."

"You don't want to see me anymore?" Peyton felt as if a knife had just been sunk into her heart.

"Peyton…things are just moving too fast."

Peyton shook her head, and despite her best efforts, a single tear escaped from her eyelids. She wiped it away with the back of her hand. *Why was he doing this? Had she really been so far off the mark? Why couldn't he let her in his heart?*

"Peyton, please say something," Malik begged.

A horn honked outside. Walking over to the window, Peyton pulled the silk curtains back and saw a taxi waiting on the street. "The cab's here."

"Call me when you get home, please?" Malik said, gulping the last bit of wine.

Peyton nodded, grabbed her satchel and unlocked the door, but something held her back. She turned and stared deep into Malik's eyes, hoping he'd beg her to stay, beg her not to walk out the door. But he didn't, and so she quietly closed the door behind her.

As he watched the taxi pull away, Malik realized that he was letting the best thing that had happened to him slip through his fingers because he wasn't capable of getting close to anyone. Had Joe Johnson damaged him from ever loving and being loved by another person? Malik threw the empty wineglass across the room and it smashed into the fireplace, shattering into tiny little pieces.

Chapter 13

"I feel like a fool," Peyton told Amber as she sobbed on her couch the following evening. They were in their pajamas and had already finished off a small cheese pizza and half a tub of Ben and Jerry's ice cream. "I bought his save-the-world routine, hook, line and sinker." She'd fallen hard for Malik. A man who didn't want her love. Was she really so desperate for comfort and affection after David's death that she had fallen for the first man that had shown any interest in her?

Amber handed Peyton another Kleenex so Peyton could blow her nose. "I warned you about trying to save wounded birds."

"Thanks a lot, Amber."

"No, seriously. Don't be so hard on yourself, Peyton. What makes you so unique is your ability to open up your heart and give so freely. You're not as closed off as the rest of us. You're kind and giving, and if Malik Williams can't see that, then it's his loss."

"Well said," Peyton said, sniffling.

"Give it time," Amber said. "He isn't the only fish in the sea."

"But he's the only fish I want," Peyton sobbed.

Amber laughed. "Oh, how I love you, Peyton." She pulled her best friend into a hug. "And I will get you through this. Scouts honor." She crossed her fingers over her heart.

"Q, what are you doing here?" Malik asked when Quentin stopped by the center at midweek and found him, along with most of the administrative team, in a temporary office setup in the gymnasium.

"Dante told me you were down and out the last couple of days, so I thought I'd come and check on you— see how things were coming along with the renovation," Quentin replied, stepping over the extension cords that were running along the floor to the outlets. "Miss Theresa." He passed by the older woman who was on the phone and gave her a kiss on the cheek. Theresa smiled back at him.

"As you can see," Malik said, motioning around the room, "we've been displaced. They've already started painting the administrative offices, but we had to keep Loretta up front."

"When will they be done?" Quentin asked. "And do they need any help?" Quentin was willing to pitch in if it meant the crew would get done quicker.

"No, no, no, they're fine. Richard's hired the best. And the contractor assembled a fine team of painters. The painters have already done the first coat and are working on the second, which should be done by the end of the day."

"What about the floors?" Quentin asked, sitting down on the last step of the gymnasium bleachers. The entire reception and administrative office floors were ripped up.

"The carpet and tile will be done over the weekend. And then they'll touch up painting, once we're all moved back in."

"Sounds like everything is going swimmingly," Quentin replied, rubbing his goatee.

Malik wished he could say the same about every facet of his life. He hadn't spoken with Peyton since she'd left his apartment in the middle of the night. Half a dozen times he'd picked up the phone to call her, but what could he say? She wanted more than he could give.

"And Peyton?" Quentin asked.

Malik rose from his seat and climbed up to the top of the bleachers to keep people from listening to his private business. Quentin followed and sat down next to him.

"Did you guys have a fight?" Quentin queried.

"We're taking a break," Malik replied. "Peyton's been pressuring me into talking about my past, and then wanting me to meet her folks. And she accused me of not letting her in, of being closed off emotionally."

Quentin nodded in agreement.

"You think she's right?"

"Yes, I do," Quentin stated emphatically. "You don't let many people in, Malik."

Malik's throat began to tighten. "Why can't I leave the past in the past? Why do I have to dredge up all those painful memories?"

"Because maybe, just maybe, it's time you finally started talking about it."

Malik shook his head. "I'm just not cut out for all this relationship drama like you are, Quentin."

"I think you're doing yourself and Peyton a disservice," Quentin responded, "if you don't see where this leads…" It was time Malik stopped running and faced his past. "I remember how hard it was for Dante and me to connect with you when we were kids. You were angry and you didn't trust anyone. But eventually, in time you let us in. But that was different. We were your boys and we had each other's backs then, but we're not your girlfriend."

"That's certainly true." Malik laughed.

"I know that might be hard for you to admit," Quentin said. "It was just as hard for me to admit that Avery was the one. But you've never been with a woman for this long. There has to be something more there."

"Such as?"

"Love. Have you ever considered that you've fallen for Peyton, which is why it's so hard for you to open up?"

Malik's brow furrowed. "Love, no. It's definitely not that. I care for Peyton, but I don't think I even know what love is." Outside of his love for Quentin, Sage and Dante, Malik hadn't known love.

"Ah, Malik, my friend," Quentin wrapped his arm around Malik's shoulder, "you're in deep denial. That's why I know you've got it bad."

"If you say so."

"I do," Quentin replied, because he saw it in Malik's eyes; he was in love with Peyton.

"Oh, Peyton, your place is fantastic," her mother stated when she walked into her daughter's apartment on Thursday morning. "The hardwood floors, the big windows that give plenty of light. It's really quite a find, my dear."

"If you discount that it's in Brooklyn and my job is in Midtown Manhattan," Peyton replied, "then yes, it's great." She'd tried to maintain a cheery outlook, even though she felt bleak. She hadn't the heart to tell her parents or Jude about her breakup with Malik.

"But the amount of space you get, honey, is priceless," her father commented.

Peyton smiled. Her parents looked no different than they had a few months before when she'd left Cleveland. Her mother was just as beautiful as ever, with salt-and-pepper hair and a smooth complexion. Her father was equally handsome in Peyton's eyes. Listening to her father's rendition of "My Funny Valentine" on his saxophone was enough to bring anyone to tears.

"It's a good thing you're staying here," Jude said, bringing the suitcases into the apartment. "My studio is no bigger than this living room, and I pay a mint. But it's close to the action."

Lydia smiled. "We wouldn't expect any less of you, Jude. You know your father and I are dying to see your play later this evening." She'd finally accepted that her baby boy was an actor. If he was happy, that was all that mattered to her.

"But first I'm going to show you all around Manhattan, and then later we'll come back and change before Jude's play," Peyton said.

"Sounds great," her parents replied in unison.

"Well, I have to get to rehearsal." Jude kissed his mother's cheek and hugged his father. "Thanks for brunch. I'll see you all tonight." He waved and was out the door.

Peyton spent the afternoon showing her parents the sights of the Big Apple: the Empire State Building, Rockefeller Center and the Metropolitan Museum of Art. Afterwards, they enjoyed a prix fixe three-course dinner in Times Square before seeing Jude's show. Her parents hadn't mentioned Malik, which was a good thing; but the next morning Peyton's luck ran out.

"Good morning, sweetheart," her mother said, entering the kitchen as she rubbed sleep from her eyes. She kissed Peyton on the cheek. "Mmm, the coffee smells great."

"It's hazelnut. How'd you sleep?"

"Wonderful," her mother said, grabbing one of the cups Peyton had set out and pouring herself some coffee.

"I hope you don't mind sitting in on my class today." Peyton flipped over the ham-and-cheese omelets she was preparing on the gas stove. "I have one later this afternoon."

"Of course not, darling," her mother said. "I'd love to see you in action."

"Good. Then I can show you NYU's campus."

"And does our day include a stop at the community center?" her mother asked. "I'm dying to meet your beau, Malik."

"Umm, I'm not sure about that." Peyton kept her back to her mother. She busied herself finishing her parents' omelets, then began making one for herself. "He's really busy right now, remodeling the center."

"Oh, that doesn't matter." Her mother came behind her, rubbing her back. "I don't mind roughing it. It's not like you and I haven't done it before, like when we helped Habitat for Humanity."

Peyton sighed. There was no way she was going to get around it; after she'd raved about Malik, her parents wanted to meet him. "Why don't we see how the day goes?" Peyton didn't turn around when she spoke.

"And how are my ladies this fine morning?" Her father came into the kitchen looking clean and fresh in a polo shirt and pressed khaki pants.

"Oh, we're just fine," Peyton answered. She slid her omelet onto a plate and put two slices of bread in the toaster.

"We're sitting in on one of Peyton's classes, and then we'll be meeting her new beau," her mother gushed.

"Hmm, sounds good to me." Her father headed straight for the coffee and poured himself a cup.

After breakfast the morning flew by. Her parents attended her afternoon lecture and toured the campus. While they took a break at Washington Square Park, her mother inquired, "Is now a good time to stop by the center?"

Peyton had dreaded this moment since they'd arrived, but she had no choice, she had to play along. She'd gotten herself into this mess, but how in hell was she going to get herself out of it? "Of course."

Peyton entered the Harlem Community Center with trepidation. She hadn't seen Malik since she'd walked out on him, and he hadn't called her either. How would he react to their showing up unannounced? Would he come out and meet her parents? If not, she would have a lot of explaining to do.

"This is it," she said, swinging open the front door.

Peyton found the reception area completely redone. The floors had been stripped of the tattered, worn carpet and replaced with multicolored Berber carpeting that could easily hide stains. The walls had been repainted in a warm tan color, far from the original faded antique white. New upholstered chairs, classy lamps and sleek brown coffee tables were sprinkled throughout.

"Looks like the remodeling is coming along nicely," her mother commented as she and Peyton's father came in behind her.

Peyton introduced her parents to Loretta. "Hi, Loretta, is Malik in his office?

"If you want to call the gymnasium his office, then yes," Loretta responded. "Go on back, Peyton."

They stepped around the carpenter that was inside the hallway gluing down the carpet, and headed to the gymnasium. She found Malik, Theresa and several other staff members in the gym. He looked as handsome as ever in jeans and a T-shirt. As soon as he saw her, he rose from his chair and walked towards them.

"Malik Williams, this is my mom and dad, Lydia and Ron Allen," Peyton said. She was shocked speechless when he pulled her into an embrace and lightly brushed his lips across hers. Peyton was momentarily taken aback and stared up at him.

"Hey." Malik smiled down at Peyton to reassure her, gazing into her eyes. He could see the anxiety lying in those brown depths. It was obvious she hadn't had a chance to tell her parents about their breakup. Being this close to her reminded Malik just how much he missed her. "It's a pleasure to meet you, Mr. and Mrs. Allen." He extended his hand to Peyton's father.

Her father returned his handshake and said, "You too. We've heard a lot about you. And might I say, this is quite an operation you have, son."

Malik nodded in agreement. "You have no idea. Has Peyton shown you around?" he asked, lightly touching the center of her back.

Peyton wasn't sure what to make of Malik's behavior. *Isn't that what she wanted him to do?* So why did it disturb her how easily he could fall into the boyfriend role? Had he been acting with her too?

"No, not yet," Peyton said, turning to Malik. She tried to read his face, but couldn't.

"Why don't I give you a tour of the facilities?" Malik walked them towards the exit. "There's a lot to see."

Malik showed Peyton and her parents the Olympic-size swimming pool and pointed out the adjacent, remodeled locker room, the computer and game rooms, and then brought them to the kitchen.

"It's not much," Malik commented. "But as soon as we get the permits we'll be knocking out that wall—" he pointed to the back wall "—and expanding it to accommodate more people. We'll also be adding a food pantry."

"Not many centers have one." Lydia Allen didn't miss a beat.

"I know, which is why I wanted one," Malik replied. "It'll be small and run during the evening by volunteers who take donations."

"I'm impressed." Her mother smiled.

"Let me show you our true gem," Malik replied. He walked them outside and over to the separate entrance for the free clinic attached to the center.

"A health clinic?" Lydia sounded surprised.

Malik nodded. "That's right, and it's free." He opened the door and allowed them to precede him. The clinic's reception area was half full of patients waiting to be seen. Malik waved to the receptionist.

"This is wonderful, Malik," Peyton's mother gushed.

"We're very happy to provide health care for those who can't afford health insurance. And we couldn't do it without the doctors who generously donate their time and services."

"I can't believe you're the director of this entire operation."

"And several centers in Manhattan," Peyton added. She was proud of the work he did.

"Malik, can you join us for dinner tonight?" her father asked. "My treat."

"I'm sure Malik is busy, Dad." Peyton wasn't sure she could share a meal with him with all this politeness between them.

"It's no problem," Malik replied. "I'd love to come, Mr. and Mrs. Allen." Malik turned to Peyton. "Why don't we go to Sylvia's, here in Harlem? They've got great soul food."

"That sounds great." Her father rubbed his belly. "I could use some down-home cooking."

"I have to finish up here first. Can I meet you there in about an hour?"

"Sure," Peyton said, then added, "I'm sure you have a lot to do." She needed to get away from Malik for her own peace of mind. "Mom, Dad, there's a bookstore nearby where we can kill some time."

"Lead the way," her mother replied.

Before Malik walked back inside, he pulled Peyton to him and kissed her again. It was unexpected and brought the same fire to Peyton's belly as all his other kisses. *How is it he could still get her all hot and bothered, when she was so angry with him?*

"I can see why you're head over heels," her mother said as he departed. "He's a dreamboat." Her mother patted Peyton on the back.

Peyton shrugged. *If she only knew.*

Dinner was filled with an uneasy tension, as Malik sat next to Peyton, playing the role of dutiful boyfriend. Although she appreciated the effort, she knew he was only doing it for her parents' benefit. He didn't mean any of it. He was ready to toss her out like yesterday's trash.

As they sat enjoying their peach cobbler and vanilla

ice cream, her mother homed in on Malik and finally got personal. "Malik, so tell us about yourself. We've been talking about ourselves way too much."

Malik bunched his shoulders and reached for his water glass. "There's not much to tell, Mrs. Allen. Along with several of my close friends, I grew up in an orphanage. After that, I went to NYU and went on to get my MBA."

Peyton noticed how cryptic Malik was about his childhood, but her parents didn't seem to catch on.

"You had to overcome quite a lot at an early age," her mother stated. "And yet, look at what you've done with yourself. I'm sure that's what my daughter sees in you." Her mother nudged Peyton knowingly. "She's done nothing but rave about you for weeks. Could we be hearing wedding bells sometime soon?" her mother asked, teasingly.

Peyton lowered her head. She wished she could crawl under the table and die of embarrassment.

"Well, uh, I…" Malik stuttered. "Mrs. Allen, really… we're nowhere near that yet."

Lydia Allen glanced at her daughter and then back to Malik. Her daughter had a strained expression, while Malik looked as if he was ready to break out in a cold sweat. Clearly, she had misread their relationship. "Oh, I'm sorry I misspoke."

"No, no, no." Malik patted Peyton's hand. "You haven't. I think the world of your daughter."

Just not the kind you want to marry, Peyton thought. "Wow, look at the time." She glanced down at her watch. It was well past ten.

Luckily, her mother took the cue. "Oh, I'm so sorry, Malik. You've worked all day and we've kept you out so late."

"I didn't mind," Malik replied. "I enjoyed myself."

"So did we," her father said, and signaled to the waitress for the bill. Once it was settled, Malik caught a cab for the Allens.

Once a taxi came curbside, Malik shook Mr. Allen's hand, but Mrs. Allen gave him a hug instead. "Thanks for dinner. We had a great time."

"It was great meeting you," Lydia said. She slid inside the cab and her husband followed.

Peyton and Malik stood awkwardly at the curb. When it seemed that Malik wasn't going to speak, Peyton finally broke the silence. "Well, thanks for coming." She leaned forward and gave him a quick hug.

"You're welcome," he whispered in her ear.

Peyton pulled away and climbed into the cab. As they drove off, Peyton decided not to look back.

Chapter 14

Peyton was quiet on the ride back to her apartment. Tonight she'd felt as if things were still unfinished between her and Malik. She needed to talk to him and find out where she stood.

She retired to her room and began to undress. She'd just finished washing off her makeup and was reaching for a face towel when she noticed her mother standing in the doorway.

"So, do you want to tell me what that was all about?"

Peyton dried her face, threw the towel down and reached for her moisturizer on the counter. "What do you mean?" she asked, pouring a generous amount into her palm.

"C'mon, Peyton. You could cut the tension at the table tonight with a knife. What's going on? I thought you were crazy about Malik."

"I am." Peyton massaged several dollops of moisturizer onto her face. "I'm just not sure that he's as crazy about me."

Her mother shook her head. "I disagree. The man I saw tonight is in love."

"Then why," Peyton asked turning around, "is it so hard for him to let me in? I know he had a painful childhood, Mama, but he won't open up to me."

"I didn't say he knows he's in love," her mother said, lightly stroking her daughter's cheek. "It's hard for men to be vulnerable. You just have to stick in there and show him you're not going anywhere. Maybe he's used to people coming and going in his life. He did say he lived in an orphanage."

"Yes, but there's something more, I'm positive of it."

"Then be patient. All will be revealed in due time."

Should she continue to stand by Malik's side until he realized he couldn't live without her? That was the question that haunted Peyton as she drifted off to sleep.

As he stood on the balcony having a Dirty Martini, Malik didn't know why he'd agreed to come with Quentin and Avery over to Richard King's for dinner. He supposed he'd accepted to keep himself busy so he wouldn't think about Peyton, but he'd done nothing else for the last two weeks. His mind would wander to her creamy, mocha skin and how soft it felt to his touch, or he'd remember the way she tilted her head to the side when she laughed. Or the way she moaned when she was on the verge of coming.

"Malik!"

Malik heard his name being called in the midst of his reverie, and he looked up. "Hmm?"

"Didn't you hear me calling you?" Quentin stared at Malik, but his friend looked like he was a million miles away.

Malik shook his head. "I'm sorry, I didn't hear you."

"Dinner is ready."

Malik followed Quentin inside and found that Richard, his wife, Cindy, and Avery were already seated at the dining room table.

"Glad you could join us," Richard said when he arrived.

"Sorry," Malik mumbled to everyone.

The butler served chilled shrimp to start, followed by herb-crusted salmon, jasmine rice and steamed asparagus. Although everything looked and smelled divine, Malik hardly tasted it. He wanted to call Peyton, but how could he, when he was the one who had broken her heart? No, it was better this way, better they'd made a clean break. He'd done his part with her parents and now they could go their separate ways. He would have to find someone to cover her mentoring at the center, however, because Malik wasn't sure he could take seeing her week in and week out.

"How's the renovation coming?" Richard inquired.

"Just fine," Malik answered. "The reception area and the administrative offices are complete. Now the contractor's tackling the computer room and the gymnasium."

"Has he received the permit for the kitchen?"

Malik shook his head. "Any day now. He's hoping to have it completed in time for Thanksgiving, so we can feed more people."

"I'd love to pitch in and help," Avery said.

Quentin and Malik both looked at her. They'd never known Avery to want to get her hands dirty. "With the ordering and preparation," she clarified.

"Now that makes more sense, my darling," Quentin said, lovingly pecking her cheek.

Avery slapped him on the shoulder. "Manual labor isn't really my forte, but I can pitch in you know."

Malik chuckled and reached for his nearly empty martini glass. "Wouldn't dream of it, Avery. I think your talents are best served behind the scenes." He finished off the martini and set it on the table. Like clockwork, the butler appeared with a fresh one. "Thank you," Malik told the butler, putting another to his lips.

From across the table, Quentin watched as Malik put away several martinis. Although he didn't act intoxicated, it was a good thing he'd driven because Malik was in no shape to drive.

"In addition to feeding the homeless, we'll have our annual turkey giveaway," Malik continued.

"Do you ever stop helping the disenfranchised?" Richard asked.

"No. Do you ever stop building an empire?" Malik queried.

"Touché." Richard lifted his wine glass. He'd found someone just as dedicated as he was. "To Malik Williams."

"To Malik." They all lifted their glasses.

As they drank to his service to the community, Malik wished he had someone to share the moment with. He wished he had Peyton.

Quentin drove Malik home later that evening and nearly had to carry him up the stairs of his brownstone. He was fumbling in Malik's leather jacket, looking for his keys, when Avery stuck her head out of the passenger window.

"Do you need some help?" Avery asked, shivering. It was awfully chilly out.

"I've got them," Quentin yelled back from the landing after producing the keys. He slid one of Malik's arms over his shoulder and carried him up the flight of stairs.

Once inside, Quentin helped Malik to his bedroom

and watched him fall onto the bed. *Poor fool,* thought Quentin. Malik didn't realize he was besotted with Peyton until after he'd broken up with her. Malik *would* have to learn the hard way.

"Are you going back to the center today?" Amber asked after their weekly educational department meeting had ended.

"Why wouldn't I?" Peyton asked as she walked to her office for some herbal tea.

"Well…I don't know. Perhaps you don't want to run into the man that just kicked you to the curb, but maybe that's just me."

"I won't disappoint the girls that I mentor. I made a commitment and I'm going to keep it."

"That's very noble of you, Saint Peyton," Amber replied, taking a seat. "But not very wise. Think about how you're going to feel if you see Malik with another woman."

Peyton stopped midstep. She hadn't thought about that. She would die inside if she saw Malik with someone else. "Maybe you're right. But I should at least finish out the rest of the year, and then the center can find someone new."

"All right." Amber had forgotten how stubborn Peyton could be. "It's your funeral."

After Amber left, Peyton returned to preparing for her next class. She was deep into research when her office phone rang.

"Hello?"

"Peyton Sawyer, please," a feminine voice said from the other line.

"This is Dr. Sawyer."

There was a short pause before the woman spoke. "Peyton, this is…Sage Anderson, one of Malik's friends.

I don't know if you remember me, we met once at Dante's."

"Oh, yes, I remember you," Peyton replied. "What can I do for you?"

"Well, Malik asked me to call. He mentioned that you were spearheading Sister-to-Sister, and he thought that, after everything that happened, it might be easier if someone else took over mentoring the girls."

"You mean, after he broke up with me?"

"Yes," Sage reluctantly admitted. "I was trying for delicacy."

"Don't bother," Peyton replied, fuming on the other end. *How dare Malik try to get rid of me!* "You can tell Malik that I—" And then a brilliant idea hit Peyton. Perhaps Sage knew about Malik's past and could shed some light on why he was trying to cut her out of every aspect of his life. So she changed her tune. "Listen, Sage, I'm not upset with you. I know Malik put you up to this."

"Thank you." Sage sighed. "I feel terrible for calling."

"Could we talk over a cup of coffee later today?" Peyton queried. "You know, about the program."

Sage's voice became light. "Okay, there's a coffee shop in my office building. But I'm busy until about six-thirty."

"That's fine. I'll meet you there." Peyton hung up after Sage supplied her with directions. Maybe now she'd finally get the answers to the questions that Malik refused to give her.

At six-thirty sharp, Sage Anderson strutted into the Starbucks in her building in a power-red pantsuit, three-inch heels and a Fendi purse. Peyton thought Sage was a knockout.

Peyton rose when she came forward and extended her hand. "Sage, thank you for meeting me. Would you care for anything to drink?" Peyton had already ordered herself a chai tea.

"No, thank you," Sage replied and sat down at the table.

"I brought some of the ideas I had for Sister-to-Sister." Peyton pulled out a folder and slid it towards Sage. "If you'd like to assist me, that would be great, then you could take over next year."

Sage smiled, revealing perfectly white teeth. "C'mon, Peyton, it's just us girls. Why don't you tell me why I'm really here?"

Was she that transparent? Apparently so.

"Malik broke up with me because he claimed our relationship was moving too fast, but I don't think that's the real reason, Sage. He's never liked discussing his past, and I've always felt like he was keeping something from me. I know I'm right."

"I see." As she looked across the table at Peyton, Sage wanted to kick Malik. This woman genuinely cared for him and Malik was acting like a complete and utter jerk. "So you're hoping I'd fill in the details?"

Peyton nodded. "I know I'm putting you in a terrible position by asking you to betray Malik's confidence, but I wouldn't ask if I didn't care, and if I didn't think I could help."

"You mean, if you didn't love him?" Sage returned.

Peyton opened her mouth to protest, but closed it since it was true. She *did* love him.

"I can tell," Sage replied, patting Peyton's hand. "And only because you love him am I going to tell you what happened. I just pray Malik will forgive me for this."

Peyton scooted her chair closer.

"Malik was physically abused by his stepfather."

"No." Peyton was horrified.

"And his mother did nothing to stop it, because she was abused as well. Child Protective Services stepped in when he was ten and took him from their care. For two years, Malik was moved in and out of foster homes."

"How horrible," Peyton gasped.

"The abuse had a terrible effect on Malik and turned him into an angry kid that no one wanted to keep. Eventually, he was placed in the same orphanage as Quentin, Dante and me, which is where he stayed until turning eighteen."

"And his mother?"

"He never saw her again. She didn't even show up at the hearing that permanently placed him with the state."

Peyton's hand flew to cover her mouth. "How could a mother do that?"

Sage shook her head. "I don't know. I can only assume the nightmares are because his stepfather Joe Johnson came to HCC a while ago, saying he wanted to donate his services to renovate the center. I'm sure that's when all those old memories started to resurface. He's always been afraid if anyone knew the truth, he would seem weak, vulnerable."

Peyton nodded as she thought about Malik's silences.

"So, now that you know, what are you going to do with this information?" Sage queried.

"I'm going to fight for him, that's what. Malik Williams is not going to get rid of me that easily." Now that she was armed with knowledge, Peyton knew what she needed to do.

Sage smiled. "A woman after my own heart."

"Why are you walking around here like someone stole your bike?" Theresa asked as they put the office back together. Malik had been moping around for the last few weeks. She'd thought he'd be happy that the renovation was going well.

They'd finally received the permit for the kitchen, and the work was progressing smoothly. The kitchen would be ready in time for their big Thanksgiving dinner, and they'd all received new furniture, courtesy of the King Corporation.

"What are you talking about?" Malik asked from near the floor, as he connected several computer plugs into the outlet.

"You've been miserable to work with lately," Theresa replied. "Cheer up, ol' boy, the offices are finally done."

"I am excited." Malik sat up. "Can't you tell?"

"Sure." Theresa laughed derisively as she turned back around to her task. She put several books onto his new built-in shelving units.

Malik knew exactly what Theresa was talking about. He'd come up with the not-so-brilliant plan of asking Sage to take over Peyton's mentoring session. He thought he'd made Sage feel sufficiently guilty for not giving enough back to the center, now that she was a successful attorney. Then last night, Sage called and said she'd been assigned to some big case, and it would require all of her attention.

So he and Peyton would continue to run into each other, it was unavoidable.

"Did you hear what I said?" Theresa asked.

"Huh?"

"I said several supermarkets have donated free turkeys. We should have about one hundred turkeys to give away."

"That's great!" Malik gave Theresa a weak "Whoopee."

Theresa glanced back at Malik, *now if only he meant*

it. Theresa would have to see about putting a smile back on Malik's face, and she knew just how to do it.

Peyton ran into Kendra at the community center on her way to her college preparatory meeting. "Kendra, what are you doing here?"

"I thought I'd finally start volunteering," Kendra said. "Malik found me a part-time job at a bookstore up the street. So, between the job and government funds, I can finally pay for day care without any help from Omar."

"Kendra, that's wonderful news."

Peyton was thrilled for her student. She was glad everything was going right for someone besides herself.

"I can only volunteer one day a week, but it's a start."

"Good for you." Peyton patted her shoulder. "Have you heard from Omar?"

"Surprisingly, no," Kendra replied. "Since he showed up at NYU, I haven't seen or heard a word from him. It was unlike Omar to at least not try and see his daughter."

"I guess no news is good news."

"That's how I'm looking at it, Dr. Sawyer. I'll see you in class." Kendra waved goodbye and headed down the hall.

Peyton smiled as she walked towards the lounge. She couldn't recall a time when she'd seen the girl look happier. Perhaps her interference had helped after all.

The day of the turkey giveaway, Malik had a small tent erected outside of the center's playground area to allow residents of the community to come and get a free turkey. Everyone in the office would take turns standing outside in the thirty-degree weather. Theresa had the first shift and Malik would be relieving her. When he arrived, she knew he was in a brooding mood. Luckily, Theresa had the cure for what ailed him.

Malik came towards Theresa carrying two steaming cups of hot chocolate. "Here you go." He handed Theresa a cup.

"Why, thank you." Theresa accepted the beverage. "You know, an old lady such as myself can't take these cold temperatures."

"Oh, please," Malik replied. "You're not old. You're going to go kicking and screaming to your grave."

"Well, today I feel old. But I've brought reinforcements." Theresa nodded towards the tent opening.

Malik turned around and found Peyton standing in the tent doorway. She was bundled up in a wool coat with a cashmere scarf wrapped around her neck, but that didn't mean that Malik had forgotten how sexy she looked underneath all those clothes.

Malik swung back around to face Theresa, but the little devil had already sneaked inside to the warmth of the center. He was going to strangle her.

"Hi," Peyton said, and smiled when she approached. "I heard you needed help handing out turkeys." Peyton unwrapped the scarf from around her neck. When Theresa called, Peyton had jumped at the chance. Malik needed to know that she knew the truth and wasn't going anywhere.

Malik sighed. "She really shouldn't have done that. The center staff could have taken care of it."

Peyton shrugged. "Well, I'm here now." She swept past him and came inside the tent.

Malik was about to comment, when several local residents came up for a free turkey. So he had no choice but to allow her to stay. But that didn't mean he wasn't uneasy standing beside Peyton. In the small quarters, he could smell the sweet scent of her perfume and it was making him dizzy with longing. It reminded him of how good they were together, in and out of bed. *And how good we could be again,* an inner voice told him.

"Malik, can you hand me a turkey?" Peyton asked. She had a gentleman standing in front of her.

"I can't do this." Malik fled form the tent and rushed inside the building.

Peyton smiled when he sent the center's business manager, Greg Burns, to cover for him. She'd gotten to him—which meant there was still hope that they could work things out.

After the cooler was bare and all the turkeys had been handed out, Greg and Peyton packed up the tent. When she was done, Peyton went inside to find Malik. It was time they finally had it out.

Before she could get a word in edgewise, Loretta pointed to the back. "He's in the kitchen with the contractor."

"Thanks, Loretta."

Peyton found Malik and another gentleman looking over the drawings. The remodeling of the kitchen had gone well. The new stainless-steel gas ranges, commercial refrigerators with swinging doors and double-decker ovens would feed quite a few people, Peyton knew. "I thought a light switch was included on that wall in the specs," she heard Malik say.

"No. If you look here—" Logan pointed to the drawing "—it wasn't on the plans."

"Can we add it?" Malik inquired.

"Sure," Logan said, "I'll have the electrician back here tomorrow."

"Thanks, Logan." Malik glanced at the doorway and saw Peyton, but he ignored her and continued his conversation. "I sure do appreciate all the hard work you and your men have put in to ensure we can open up the kitchen for Thanksgiving dinner."

"It was my pleasure. You guys do good work here." Logan nodded at Peyton on his way out.

"Malik, we need to talk," Peyton said, walking towards him.

"There's nothing to talk about." Malik turned his back on Peyton and started rolling up the construction drawings.

"Malik." Peyton touched his shoulder. "I know the truth."

Malik whirled around and stared at her. "And what do you *think* you know?"

Peyton was quiet for several moments. She'd come this far, she had to finish. "I know about Joe Johnson. I know what kind of man he is—and was to you and your mother. I know that he hurt you."

Malik was dumbfounded as Peyton confirmed that she knew his deepest, darkest secret. *How did she find out? Who could have told her?* Malik ran his fingers through his dreads. Not many people knew that he'd been abused. He couldn't imagine that any one of his friends or even Andrew would have betrayed him.

"I'm sorry for what happened to you, Malik. I'm sorry that Joe took away your childhood from you. And I just want you to know that this information doesn't change the way I feel about you," Peyton continued, even though Malik stood there staring at her with cold and unfathomable eyes. "What happened was horrible, criminal, Malik. You were just a child and couldn't protect yourself. I just wish you felt you could confide in me."

"I couldn't!" Malik yelled. "I didn't want to talk about it. And I don't want to talk about it now. Why couldn't you have leave well enough alone?"

Suddenly unsure, her voice quavered. "I'm sorry. I was just trying to help."

"Well, you're not. You should have left the past in the past."

"That's bull, Malik," Peyton responded. "The past has been staring you in the face for weeks. Don't you think you need to deal with it?"

"Who are you to tell me what I should do?"

"I'm the woman who loves you," Peyton said passionately. Her eyes blazed with fire as they held his.

Malik was stunned by Peyton's declaration.

"You may not believe my love is here to stay," Peyton replied, "because the one person who should have loved you unconditionally withheld her love. But I'm going to show you I'm different. I'm not going anywhere, Malik. I'm going to fight for us. I will not let your fear or the past get in the way, because I believe we have something special." Peyton grabbed both sides of Malik's face.

Malik shook his head free and darted his eyes to avoid looking at Peyton. If he did, he might lose himself in her beautiful brown eyes. "You're wrong."

"Believe me," Peyton said, and reached up to pull Malik's head towards her. She pressed her mouth and body against his. The kiss was all softness and gentleness at first; but Malik couldn't resist the pull, and he invaded her mouth with his tongue.

Peyton's lips parted as he probed the recesses of her mouth. Her entire body came alive at his kiss. She could hear her breathing becoming uneven, feel her breasts rapidly rising and falling. She wanted him. Her hands moved restlessly across Malik's back and she clung to him, eager for more—and he supplied it. His tongue went deep into her mouth with one long hard thrust, as though he wanted to take her right then and there. There was no other way to describe the way his nimble tongue penetrated her mouth so thoroughly, so completely.

While his tongue worked magic with her mouth, his hands caressed her face and tangled inside her hair, pulling her even closer to him. A ribbon of desire slowly coiled through Peyton and she forgot her surroundings until they both heard a sound.

"Ahem." It was Logan, standing in the doorway. "Malik, when you have a minute, I'd like to talk to you up front." Logan smiled knowingly before walking away.

Slowly, Malik released Peyton. "That shouldn't have happened." He inhaled, forcing air into his lungs.

"Yes, it should have," Peyton said, caressing his cheek. She just couldn't understand his resistance. "I have to go too. But know this, Malik Williams, it isn't over between us—not by a long shot." Peyton sauntered out of the room leaving a shaken Malik in her wake.

Chapter 15

"I don't know what happened," Malik told Dante and Quentin later that evening, when they all met up for a game of pool. "One minute, I'm furious with her because someone told her about Joe, and the next minute I'm kissing her like she's the last woman on earth, right in the middle of the kitchen. All because one of you fools—" Malik tossed a cue stick at Quentin "—let it slip."

"Let *what* slip?" Dante asked.

"About Joe."

"We," Quentin pointed to Dante and then to himself, "didn't tell Peyton anything about your past. We would never break your confidence."

Malik stared at him in confusion. He'd already spoken with Andrew, who assured him he'd remained mum. "So, if it wasn't you guys and it wasn't Theresa, then who was…"

"Sage," Dante and Quentin said in unison.

"She wouldn't." Malik shook his head.

"She would if she thought it was in your best interest," Quentin returned.

Malik threw the cue stick down on the table. "I'm going to strangle her."

"What are you so mad about, anyway?" Dante asked. "The truth is out there. Now you and Peyton can move on."

"Exactly," Quentin concurred.

"What makes you think I want to move on with her?"

"Do you recall kissing her like she was the last woman on earth, even though you're upset with her?" Dante inquired.

"And you can't get her out of your mind, no matter how hard you try?" Quentin added. He recalled a similar feeling when he was falling for Avery. "You got drunk at Richard's the other night just because you missed her."

Malik didn't answer.

"I rest my case," Dante replied.

"Whose case I need to get on right now is Sage's," Malik replied. "This time our little sister has gone too far."

The next morning, Malik marched into Greenberg, Hanson, Waggoner and Associates to meet with Sage and give her a piece of his mind. He'd had all night to think, and the more he did, the angrier he got.

"Sage Anderson, please," he asked the receptionist.

"Down the hall and to the left." She pointed to the corridor.

"Thank you." Sage's assistant was not at her desk, so he stormed right into her office unannounced.

Sage was sitting at her desk reading a brief, but as soon

as she saw who it was her face lit up. "Malik," Sage said and smiled, then stood up. "This is a pleasant surprise."

Malik glared at her as he closed the door behind him. "This isn't a social visit."

"Oh, dear." From the stormy look on Malik's face, she realized that he knew she'd spilled the beans to Peyton.

"Sage, I have a bone to pick with you," Malik huffed. "What possessed you to tell Peyton about Joe? You had no right to tell her my personal business."

"Someone had to," Sage answered, and folded her arms across her chest. "You were going to let a woman like Peyton—who obviously cares a great deal about you—get away. I did the right thing and I'm not ashamed of it. I'd do anything for the people I love."

"It wasn't your story to tell," Malik retorted.

"Malik, I did this for you," Sage replied. "You have to let go of the past and the anger. You should be embracing a future with Peyton, not running away from it."

"You're one to talk, Sage. When was your last serious relationship?"

He had a point. Sage did shy away from relationships, but it wasn't because she didn't want one. She just didn't have the time. "This isn't about me. It's about you." Sage pointed to Malik. "You need help. I think you should consider counseling, so you can resolve these issues."

"How dare you!" Malik roared. "You know nothing about what I went through."

"And why don't I, Malik?" Sage asked, coming towards him. "Dante, Quentin and I are the closest thing you have to family, and yet you've never really talked to us about what you went through." Sage came forward and stroked his cheek. "Sure, you told us he hit you, but that little boy inside must still be in pain. You have to heal him before you'll ever really be whole."

Malik pushed Sage's hand away. "Enough with the psychobabble, Sage. You don't know what you're talking about."

Sage knew she'd hit a nerve, because Malik was defensive. "If you came here looking for an apology," Sage said as she smoothed down her skirt, "you're not going to get one. I did it because I was trying to help you, and I'd do it again."

"Mind your own business, Sage, and stay out of my life." Malik turned on his heel and stalked out of the office.

"Should I go and talk to him?" Peyton asked Amber that evening over the phone.

"He knows you know the truth. Maybe you should give him some time to process it."

"But he needs me, Amber," Peyton responded. "The man who abused him has suddenly risen from the ashes and has been harassing him."

"And what are you going to do?" Amber inquired. "Fight off the big bad bully? Peyton, you have to allow him to deal with this in his own time."

Peyton inhaled. "I know you're right, but I just feel so helpless."

"There is nothing you can do. Malik most likely needs professional help to deal with the scars and I'm not talking about the physical ones that have since healed."

"I will suggest therapy when I see him next at the center's grand re-opening."

"So you're going?"

"Of course," Peyton responded. "It's Malik's big night. All of the top brass from the CAN are going to be there, as well as the entire center's staff and volunteers. How can I not show?"

"All right. Once your mind is made up, nothing and

no one will talk you out of it. Just be prepared that he may not be willing to hear you right now."

"That's a chance I'm willing to take," Peyton replied. She had a feeling that Malik would be powerless to resist her in the flattering cocktail dress she'd purchased that hugged all the right places. After the party, Malik Williams was going to be putty in her hands.

The night of the official unveiling of the center's renovation, Malik stood back and looked at his handiwork. He and Theresa had been running around for the last two days making sure everything was perfect for tonight's festivities.

He'd barely had enough time to run home, shower and change into a formal black business suit with a tuxedo tie shirt, before he was due back.

"The center looks fantastic, Malik." Andrew came up from behind him and smacked him on the back. The center looked modern and up-to-date. The computer room had all the latest technology and gadgets, from webcams to wireless mouses. Stainless-steel appliances replaced the old, worn-out stove, microwave and refrigerator in the kitchen, while the eating area had been enlarged by three times its normal size. They'd lost one of the three lounges, but could now feed more people during their weekly dinners. "You've done an amazing job."

Malik shook his head. "I wish I could take all the credit, but I can't. A lot of people put a lot of time and effort into seeing this project completed within a short span of time." He couldn't wait for the top brass from the Children's Aid Network, and several influential community leaders, to see the project.

"Doesn't matter." Andrew shook his head. "I'm still proud of you, son."

Malik grinned. "Thanks, Andrew."

"So am I," Theresa said, walking into the reception area. She too, had changed, and was now wearing a figure-flattering black gown, with a sheer satin shawl. "CAN is going to be very impressed with your leadership."

Theresa had checked on the caterers who were putting the finishing touches on the festive Thanksgiving decorations and who were now bringing food to several stations strategically located throughout the gymnasium. They would be serving a variety of hot and cold hors d'oeuvres, sliced meats, champagne and petit fours for dessert. Everything was going according to plan.

"Greetings, my friend!" Quentin said when he and Avery walked in. "Andrew." Quentin shook Malik's mentor's hand and kissed Theresa on the cheek. "You're looking as beautiful as ever."

"Thank you, Q," Theresa said, smiling.

Several minutes later, Dante and Sage arrived dressed in their finest evening attire. Dante looked around at the new paint, flooring and modern furniture. With his focus on the restaurant, he hadn't been by the center in a long time. "The place looks really great, Malik."

"Sure does," Avery replied.

"Couldn't have done it without you," Malik said, then leaned forward and kissed Avery's cheek. Everyone looked great. The men were in suits and the ladies in cocktail dresses.

Avery touched her face. "Thanks, Malik." She knew it wasn't easy for a man as proud as Malik to admit he needed help.

"Can I get in on the action?" Sage asked, coming towards Malik with her arms outstretched for a hug. "Or are you still mad at me?"

Malik glanced down at Sage. He knew she loved

him and only wanted the best for him. Malik found it hard to stay mad at her. "Of course you can," he said, leaning down. He lifted Sage off the floor and enveloped her in a big hug.

"Put me down." She swatted his arm.

"I love you too." Malik kissed her forehead and lowered her to the floor.

"Why don't you all go to gymnasium?" Theresa asked, as several more guests started to arrive and fill up the small reception area. "The caterer is all set up and has some scrumptious food."

"Now, this I have to see," Dante replied. Malik had offered him the catering gig, but he had passed. He'd wanted to support Malik and enjoy the night, not cook.

As they all headed towards the gymnasium, Malik glanced towards the door. Although he'd broken up with her, Malik still hoped Peyton would show. They'd shared a passionate kiss the other day, and she'd said they weren't over. *After all his rejections, had she finally had enough of him?*

Peyton glanced down at her watch. She was running late. She should have left an hour ago to get ready for the party, but she'd been caught by a student who was stressing over classes, and she had been asked to attend yet another departmental meeting.

It was late when Peyton finally left the building. She'd brought her car and paid for parking because she knew she'd need to get on the road quickly. She was nearly to the garage when she heard a noise behind her.

Peyton glanced over her shoulder and stared down the street, but didn't see anything. She had an uneasy feeling and picked up her pace so she could reach the lighted confines of the parking garage. She waved at the attendant on duty before hopping on the elevator. The ride up to the third floor was interminable and Peyton glanced anxiously at the panel display. When the elevator rung for her floor, Peyton rushed out the door and bumped into someone. "I'm sorry," she apologized, and then glanced up to find Kendra's boyfriend, Omar, staring down at her.

Peyton stepped backward. "What are you doing here, Omar?"

"It's time you and I finally got a few things straight, Professor." Omar took a threatening step towards her.

Peyton's eyes darted around for help, but the garage was deserted. She looked for the nearest exit, but the door to the stairs was to the side of her. If she ran, he'd catch her easily. "*We* have nothing to get straight," Peyton replied. She had to stand her ground. If he thought she was afraid of him, he'd move in for the kill. "This is between you and Kendra."

Peyton moved forward but Omar blocked her path.

"You're the cause of all our troubles. From day one, you've been filling Kendra's head with this Miss Independent garbage, and now she's acting like she doesn't need me no more."

Peyton stared Omar dead in the eye. "That's your issue, not mine. If you'll excuse me, I have someplace to be."

When she went to walk past him, Omar grabbed Peyton by the arm and shoved her up against the wall. "Now, did I say you could leave?"

Peyton blinked several times as the pain of her head hitting the cement wall temporarily threw her off balance.

"You're going to rough me up like you do Kendra?" Peyton asked, holding her head as she forced herself from the wall. "I warn you, Omar, if you lay another hand on me you'll end up in prison on assault charges, because I'm not like Kendra, I am not going to go away quietly."

Omar lowered his fist. "You—" Omar shoved Peyton "—need to stay out of my business, because one day you may not be so lucky." And with that warning, Omar took off towards the stairs.

Peyton heard the door close beside her as she sagged against the wall.

"You've done a fine job with this establishment, Malik," Blake Harris, president of the Children's Aid Network, said. "When we told you CAN didn't have the funds, you went out and found another source of funding. You're really an asset to the organization."

"Thank you, sir," Malik replied. "I enjoy what I do." Malik glanced at the door and saw that Richard King and his wife, Cindy, had finally arrived. "But you should meet the benefactor in person." Malik ushered him over.

"Richard King, I'd like to introduce you to Blake Harris, president of the Children's Aid Network."

"It's a pleasure to meet you," Richard said and extended his hand.

"No, the pleasure is all mine," Blake replied, shaking his hand. "Your corporation has allowed CAN to continue to help children and families in need."

"We're happy to do it," Richard replied. "Let me introduce you to my wife, Cindy."

While they finished introductions, Malik stepped away and searched through the crowd for Peyton. He ran into Quentin at one of the food stations. "Have you seen Peyton anywhere?"

"Hmm, sorry." Quentin covered his mouth. Malik had just caught him with a canapé in his mouth. "Haven't seen her."

Malik shook his head. "I don't understand it. She should be here. It's not like her not to show up."

"Aren't you the one who broke up with her?" Quentin asked.

Malik lowered his head. "Yes, I did. But that hasn't seemed to stop her." As a matter of fact, Peyton had become more stubborn. She was like a dog with a bone. Malik hated to admit it, but it was a turn-on. "I'm going to call her cell." Malik dug into his pocket for his phone and walked towards the exit.

Once he was in the hall, he dialed Peyton's number. But it went to straight to voice mail. Malik had an uneasy feeling in the pit of his stomach that something wasn't right. It wasn't like Peyton not to show up or call. She knew how important this night was to him and to the center. Peyton would show up, no matter how angry she was with him.

Theresa came out of the gymnasium in search of the caterer and found Malik pacing the hall floor.

"Theresa, I have to go," Malik stated.

"What do you mean?" Theresa asked, raising an eyebrow. "*Everyone* is here."

"I know, and you'll have to cover for me."

"And why would I do that?" Theresa asked, putting her hand on her hip.

"Because I think Peyton is in trouble and she may need me." Malik started towards the door. "Just cover for me," he called over his shoulder, and ran down the hall.

"I will," Theresa yelled at his retreating figure. She just hoped everything was okay.

Because guests were coming and going, several taxis were outside, waiting, and Malik quickly hopped into one. "NYU, please—as fast as you can."

He was at Peyton's building within thirty minutes,

but as he exited the taxi, a frog lodged in Malik's throat. A police car was parked outside of her office building.

Frantic, Malik tossed several bills at the driver and rushed towards the entrance. He took the stairs two at a time, until he reached the second floor. A police officer was standing outside Peyton's office.

"Is everything all right?" Malik asked, coming towards the cop. "Is Peyton okay?"

The officer halted him from entering. "And who are you?"

Peyton glanced up from giving her statement and saw Malik in the doorway. "It's all right. He's my boy-friend," she said, and motioned him in.

Malik didn't mind that she used the term; he was just glad she wasn't alone and that Amber was sitting with her and the cop. He didn't see any bruises, but he did notice she was holding an icepack against the back of her head.

"Thank you, I think that's enough for now," the officer said and stood up. "We'll need you to come downtown to complete that restraining order."

Peyton nodded. "Thank you."

"You're welcome," the officer said, and tipped his cap before leaving.

"What happened?" Malik asked, rushing forward and kneeling in front of Peyton.

Concern was etched across his face. Peyton smiled. *He loved her.* She was sure of it. She just wished he would say it.

"Omar attacked her in the parking garage." Amber answered his question.

"He shoved me up against a wall and I hit my head," Peyton explained. "But other than that, I'm fine. I think he only meant to scare me. He wanted to get me off his back."

"I'm going to kill him." Malik rose to his feet.

"No, you're not." Peyton also stood up. "Listen to me, Malik." She grabbed his jaw. She didn't want him getting into any trouble because of her. "You're going to let the police handle this. Now, if you'll excuse me, I have to go to the bathroom."

Once she'd left, Malik turned to Amber. "I need Kendra's number. I'm sure she knows where I can find Omar."

"Malik, I don't think that's a good idea. Peyton's right, you should stay out of this."

"I am not going to let that snot-nosed punk run roughshod over Peyton," Malik growled.

"Does your presence here mean that you're here to stay?" Amber inquired. "That it's not over between you and Peyton? Because if not, then I see no reason to help you."

Malik stared back at Amber without answering.

She took his silence as a "yes." "Okay." She grabbed Peyton's purse and pulled out her cell phone. When she found the number, she rattled it off to Malik.

"I have to go. Take Peyton home and I'll stop by later. I have business to attend to."

Malik arrived at Omar's apartment within the hour. Kendra hadn't wanted to give him the information, especially when he'd informed her that Omar had attacked her professor—but Malik had been adamant, so she relented.

The apartment was in a bad part of town, but it didn't bother Malik. Before Joe, when it had just been him and his mother, they'd lived in one hole in the wall after the other. Later, when he, Quentin, Dante and Sage had moved out of the orphanage, the four musketeers hadn't been able to afford much. He and Sage had been at NYU in work-study programs, while Dante and Quentin toiled at minimum-wage jobs for their true passions— cooking and photography.

Malik climbed the steps to Omar's apartment, hell-bent on teaching the kid a lesson. How dare he lay a finger on Peyton? He banged on the door for several minutes, but no one answered. He was about to leave when a young man walked up the stairs from the other direction. "Can I help you, playa?"

Malik stared back at the young man who was full of fire and bravado. His jeans were hanging down and his baseball cap was tipped to the side.

"Are you Omar Bishop?"

"Who wants to know?" Omar postured.

"I do." Malik punched a fist in one hand and took a threatening step towards Omar.

"Hey man, what's up?" Omar asked.

"I believe we know someone in common."

Omar looked Malik up and down. "With those threads, I doubt it, my brotha." He turned his back on Malik, pulled out his keys and unlocked the door. He was about to close the door when Malik stuck his foot out.

"Not so fast." Malik pushed the door open and forced his way inside. Omar backed away from him like a scared puppy dog. It amazed Malik that abusers could push women around so easily, but if they're picked on by someone their own size they cower.

"I don't know what you think I done," Omar began.

"You know what you did." Malik shut the door behind him. "You paid Peyton Sawyer a visit and roughed her up, didn't you?"

Omar clearly recognized the name, because Malik watched him look around the room for a weapon—as if

Malik would ever let him get the opportunity to reach for one. "I didn't…" Omar shook his head. "I didn't hit her."

"No, but you shoved her against a wall." Malik followed Omar into the living room. "Threatened her."

"I just wanted her to stop interfering in my family." Omar was so busy backing up as far as he could, that he fell onto a table. "She…she's been putting all these ideas in my girl's head, pitting her against me."

Omar tried to get up, but Malik lowered himself until he was inches away from Omar's face.

"How would you feel if someone threatened your woman?" Malik grabbed Omar by the collar and lifted him to his feet. "What would you do?" Malik pushed him against the nearby wall and held his arm against Omar's throat. There was fear in Omar's eyes, the same fear Malik had felt all those years ago when Joe used to beat him with an extension cord or choke him into submission.

"That's why you're here, isn't it? To kick my butt? Well, then—just do it!" Omar taunted Malik. "Stop playing and just do it, man. I'm used to getting my butt kicked."

Malik wanted to strike back and get revenge, but Omar's words gave him pause.

"What did you just say?"

"I said I'm used to it," Omar replied. "So go ahead."

Although Omar puffed out his chest, Malik saw tears in the young man's eyes—and for the first time, he saw a scared little boy looking back at him.

"My daddy used to beat the crap out of me and my momma every night, so if you wanna hit me, then go ahead. I know I deserve it for messing with your girl."

Malik stepped backward.

"I said *go 'head!*" Omar yelled, coming towards him.

Malik stared at Omar for a long time and then turned away. He ran his fingers through his dreads. *How had he gotten here?* He'd almost hit that kid. If he had, he'd be no better than Joe Johnson.

Malik turned and faced Omar. "I did come here to beat the living daylights out of you, but I'm not going to do it."

Omar was shocked. "Why not?"

"Because, kid, I could have been you."

"What are you talking about?"

"My stepfather used to beat the crap out of me too. But unlike you, *Omar,* I didn't turn to violence. Just now I stopped myself from becoming him, but I could just as easily have ended up like you. That's why I'm going to get you some help," Malik stated.

"I don't need any help," Omar said. "I've been taking care of myself for years."

"Everyone needs help, Omar," Malik replied. *Even me,* Malik thought. "Peyton may want to file charges against you, but I can persuade her not to—if you'll agree to go to counseling."

"You would do that?" Omar was confused. "Why would you help me? You don't even know me."

"I just will," Malik replied and started towards the door. "And don't even think about running, because if you do, I'll find you."

After he left Omar's apartment, a maelstrom of emotions overtook Malik, and he realized he needed to see Peyton. He wanted to tell her everything that had happened. He had to finally tell her that she was right. He did need someone. He needed her.

Chapter 16

Someone was knocking at her front door.

Peyton glanced at the clock on her nightstand. It was after 11 p.m. and she was in no mood for company. She had a splitting headache and had finally started to drift off to sleep. Reluctantly, she rose from her bed and padded down the hall in her slippers. When she looked through the peephole and saw Malik standing at her front door, Peyton's heart nearly leapt out of her chest. She'd thought that it was truly over between them when he'd left her office without saying a goodbye. So, why was he here?

Slowly, she unlocked the dead bolt and opened the door. "What are you doing here?" she asked, keeping the door half closed.

Malik looked down, and when his eyes finally landed on hers they were haunted. "I need you."

Peyton had been waiting for weeks to hear those words.

She held her arms open and Malik rushed into them. When he finally released her, Peyton took Malik's hand and led him to her living room couch. She held him in her arms for what seemed like hours before he finally spoke.

"I almost became my stepfather tonight. I nearly attacked Omar," Malik said. "I almost lost myself tonight."

"But you didn't." Peyton grabbed his chin and turned him towards her. "Did you?"

Malik shook his head. "No, I didn't. I stopped myself in the nick of time."

"That's because you're a good man, Malik," Peyton reassured him.

"I don't know, Peyton. I could have hurt that kid. I felt so angry that he threatened you. I wanted...I wanted to tear him to pieces. I felt all this rage inside, and I was going to take it out on him."

"Don't beat yourself up," Peyton said. "You've been through a lot—a lot that you haven't fully dealt with."

"You might be right." Malik admitted the truth for the first time. For so long, he wouldn't admit that he needed to talk to someone about the abuse he'd endured as a child—not to himself, not to his friends, not to Peyton. The orphanage had tried sending him to counseling when he was younger, but he'd acted out so much, that they'd finally dropped the matter altogether.

It warmed Peyton's heart to finally hear Malik admitting that he needed help. "I am so glad to hear you say that."

"Trust me, it's not easy for me to say, and neither is this...." Malik turned around until he was facing Peyton. "I was a fool to ever break up with you, Peyton. And I'm sorry if I hurt you. I was stubborn and pigheaded and..."

"I understand," Peyton said and slid into Malik's lap, but when she tried to kiss him, Malik resisted.

"No, wait. I have to say this." Malik put a finger to

her lips. "Peyton, I'm crazy about you. From the moment I saw you at Dante's, I knew you were special. And the more we worked together, the harder I fell for you. I tried to push you away, but I don't want to do that anymore. I'm in love with you, Peyton Sawyer."

When Malik finally hazarded a glance at Peyton, her eyes were misted with tears. "I love you too."

Peyton locked lips solidly with his. She shifted in his lap and her buttocks came into intimate contact with his bulging groin. Malik sat upright and Peyton joined him. They worked together to free each other of their clothing. He slid her robe down her shoulders and tossed it aside as Peyton feverishly unbuttoned his shirt. She wanted to revel in his broad, well-defined chest, but Malik was tugging at her nightie, so Peyton lifted her arms and, in one fluid movement, Malik had it over her head and sent it flying in the air.

Malik's eyes landed on Peyton's bare breasts, but she shook her head. Reaching down she unbuttoned his pants and eased the zipper down. Malik stood, stepped out of them and his briefs, and was back on the sofa before she had a chance to miss him.

"Come here." Peyton gripped his shoulders and fell back onto the pillows, taking Malik with her.

"I've missed you," Malik said as he lay on top of her. He caressed her face and buried his hands in her hair.

When she felt his hard length rubbing against her stomach, Peyton jerked her hips upward. "So did I. That's why I want you inside me. Now."

"I need to protect us first." Malik reached for his pants, pulled out a foil packet and quickly took care of the protection. "Are you ready for me, Peyton?"

"More than ready, baby."

Malik's hot and greedy mouth captured hers while

his hands nudged her legs apart. He drove himself deep within Peyton in one long, satiny stroke. She felt him hard and slick, pumping inside her, and Peyton couldn't resist letting out a long, satisfied moan. He was just what she wanted. Just what she needed.

Malik's dark eyes connected with Peyton's and she met him thrust for thrust by rolling her hips. He rewarded her by slowly withdrawing and plunging in again. Malik thought he would die from ecstasy as Peyton milked him by clenching her inner muscles around him and kissing him full on the lips. The pressure intensified, becoming stronger, until a tidal wave struck, imploding the world around them. As he slowly descended back down to earth, Malik realized just how much he loved Peyton and that he didn't want to ever live without her.

"So, what happened to you last night?" Andrew asked when Malik strolled into the center well after 10 a.m., with a smile on his face. Andrew was helping Theresa and the volunteers prepare for the big Thanksgiving Day dinner coming up on Thursday, putting up holiday decorations in the reception area. "The board of CAN was very shocked that you weren't here for the big speech."

"Last night... I wasn't even here to thank the King Corporation." Malik couldn't believe how negligent he'd been. All he'd thought about was Peyton and her safety. Richard King deserved a lot better. "I must have seemed really inconsiderate."

"Don't worry, I stepped in for you," Andrew replied. "We said there was a security problem at the Brooklyn property, and that you felt you had to go and check it out personally. So you may have some explaining to do this morning."

The first thing he needed to do was call Richard and

offer his apologies. "I will. Thanks, Andrew." Malik patted his shoulder. "I owe you one."

"So you never answered my question. What happened to you last night?"

"A lot."

"Care to elaborate?"

Malik motioned for Andrew to follow him into his office. Once they were inside, Malik closed the door. "I came this close—" Malik pinched his thumb and index finger together "—to going to the dark side last night, Andrew, and it scared me. It scared me so bad that I've decided to go to counseling."

"You have?" Andrew was shocked. The last time he'd mentioned it Malik nearly bit his head off.

Malik nodded. "I have. I almost hit this young kid because he'd shoved Peyton. And do you know what I realized? I realized that I'd become like Joe, and that's when I knew that something had to change. I had to deal with the past once and for all."

"You had an epiphany."

"Yes, I did. And now it's time to put that plan into action."

"I know a great therapist," Andrew replied. After years of being director of the center, he'd referred many people.

Malik turned and smiled. "Thanks, Andrew. That's just what I need."

"Are you okay, Dr. Sawyer?" Kendra asked when she poked her head into Peyton's office later that afternoon. "I heard from Malik about what happened."

Peyton nodded. So Kendra gave Malik the info he needed to go after Omar? She figured as much. Thankfully, the situation hadn't ended in disaster. Instead, it had been an impetus to propel Malik into realizing that he had a lot of unresolved issues about his stepfather's abuse that he needed to deal with.

"I'm fine, Kendra," Peyton replied, smiling. "No broken bones." She turned around so Kendra could see her.

"I'm so glad." Kendra sat down and released a huge sigh of relief. "When Malik asked me for Omar's address, I didn't know what to do, but he insisted. He didn't hurt Omar, did he?"

"No, he didn't. Malik discovered that Omar is a victim of child abuse himself and probably needs some counseling."

"Maybe that's why he's always been so angry," Kendra said. "Do you think he can be helped?"

"I certainly hope so," Peyton said. "I'll agree not to press charges, in exchange for Omar immediately going into counseling and anger management."

"That's awfully generous of you, Dr. Sawyer, but why should I be surprised? That's who you are." Kendra smiled.

"Don't canonize her yet," Amber said from the door, "otherwise, she won't be able to fit her halo inside the door."

"Dr. Martin," Kendra said, smiling, "it's good to see you." She rose from the chair. "Guess I'll get going." Kendra started towards the door, then stopped. "In case I haven't said this before, thank you, Dr. Sawyer, for all your help. You saved my life." She waved as she walked out.

"Wow, a lifesaver!" Amber teased her. "Now how are you going to outdo yourself?"

"Oh, stop." Peyton laughed.

"So, how did last night turn out?" Amber asked, sitting down in the chair Kendra vacated. After the way Malik had reacted when he'd seen Peyton hurt last night, Amber was sure he'd returned. "Did you have a visitor?"

Peyton grinned from ear to ear. "Malik stopped by

and… Amber, he loves me. He loves me as much I love him!"

"Peyton, that's fantastic!!" Amber couldn't be happier for her. She knew how deep Peyton's feelings ran for Malik. Even though she'd been skeptical initially, there was no denying the couple loved each other.

"After all these years, Amber, I've finally found love again, and everything is sunshine," Peyton sang.

As a favor to Andrew, the therapist he'd suggested squeezed Malik in for a session before he left for his four-day Thanksgiving weekend.

"How was your first visit?" Peyton asked him later, when he stopped by her office. He'd been on her mind all morning and she was anxious to hear details.

"It wasn't what I expected," Malik said, taking a seat across from her. "I thought I'd be sitting on the couch pouring my heart out, but it was nothing like that. He allowed me to talk about whatever I wanted."

"How did that make you feel?"

"Comfortable," Malik answered honestly. "We talked about how I almost lost control with Omar, and the profound effect it had on me."

Malik had insisted Omar meet him and Peyton downtown at the police station. And in front of an assistant district attorney, Peyton agreed not to press charges, provided Omar sought counseling. The assistant district attorney had some names on file, and Omar had already called to tell Malik that he'd set up his first appointment with a therapist. Omar wasn't happy about it, but he hoped it was the first step in helping him get his family back.

"And did you take anything away from the session?"

"Yes," Malik said. "I realized I have a lot of built-up anger at my mother for not protecting me from Joe's abuse and for abandoning me. The therapist said we have a lot of work to do." Malik didn't want to take his anger about his mother's abandonment and negligence, or Joe's abuse, out on another human being.

"But it's a start." Peyton walked from behind her desk and kneeled down in front of him. Malik's anger issues wouldn't be resolved overnight; she would have to stay positive and encourage him along the way.

"Yes, it is," Malik admitted. "He said one day when I'm ready, I should confront Joe about the abuse and tell him how much he hurt me."

"I think that's an important step." When she brushed back his dreads so she could see his face, Peyton saw the doubt in Malik's eyes.

"Joe's never going to admit that he did anything wrong."

"No, he probably won't," Peyton agreed. "But it might do you some good, honey, to finally say the words aloud."

"What would I do without you?" Malik asked, pulling her towards him and sitting her in his lap.

"Let's hope you never have to find out."

On Thanksgiving Day, Malik and Peyton, Andrew and Theresa, Dante and Sage, and many other community center staffers, served Harlem's homeless and residents a free Thanksgiving supper. Quentin and Avery had been unable to make it, due to a previous invitation to her parents'.

Malik was pleased with how the day was progressing. Everyone had pitched in, because the new setup had allowed several hands to be in the kitchen at one time. They would serve fried turkey, stuffing, mashed potatoes and gravy, green bean casserole and candied yams and apple and pumpkin pies donated from a local bakery.

Theresa had decorated the tables with festive centerpieces from the afterschool program, so the now-spacious dining room was filled with the Thanksgiving spirit.

"Thank you for pitching in," Malik said to Dante when he came into the kitchen looking for trash bags. Although Andrew had fried several turkeys, Dante had prepared all the sides, with some help from volunteers. He was still cooking more food, because he was afraid they'd run out.

"You don't have to thank me," Dante said as he turned on the food processor to whip more mashed potatoes. "I'm doing what I love. And, by the way—" he cut off the processor "—I have never seen you look happier, my friend."

"I don't think I've ever been this happy before," Malik replied honestly. Peyton had brought a joy to his life that he hadn't known was missing, and now Malik felt completely fulfilled.

Malik and Peyton were so busy laughing and talking as they served dinner that they didn't notice Joe Johnson, until he was standing in front of them with his Styrofoam plate held out.

"What are you doing here, Joe?" Malik asked.

"Well, I wanted to see your handiwork," Joe replied, glancing around the room. "See what all Richard King's money could buy."

"Is there a problem here?" Andrew asked from Malik's other side. He may have been carving turkey, but Andrew had no qualms about stepping in and taking over.

"There's no problem." Malik sunk his spoon into the mashed potatoes and plopped some on Joe's plate. "It *is* Thanksgiving." Malik turned to Andrew and feigned a smile.

Joe nodded. "Thanks." He slid over to Peyton. "Gravy, please."

Reluctantly, Peyton ladled some gravy onto Joe's potatoes, even though she really wanted to pour it over his head.

As Joe moved down the line to Sage for candied yams, he was greeted with the same chilly reception.

Only Andrew managed a "Happy Thanksgiving."

"I swear, that man has a lot of nerve showing his face here," Sage leaned back and whispered to Malik, once Joe had gone.

Malik nodded and watched Joe sit at one of the tables with the less fortunate. *What was he even doing here?* Malik wondered. It wasn't like he was down-and-out. The man just wanted to ruin his holiday. The more he watched Joe enjoying Thanksgiving dinner, the more Malik wanted to walk over there and wipe that smug smile off his face. The therapist had said in time he would be ready to confront Joe. Maybe now was the time.

"I'm going to talk to Joe."

"I don't know…" Peyton replied. She wasn't sure it was a good idea.

"It may not change anything, but at least I'll get it off my chest." Malik headed towards the door.

"All right, I'll cover for you."

"Are you sure that was a good idea?" Sage had overheard them talking.

Peyton nodded. "Trust me, Sage, he needs to do this."

"Okay…" Sage glanced nervously towards the door. She just hoped they wouldn't be calling for an ambulance later.

"Joe, wait!" Malik caught up with him at the side entrance.

"What do you want?" Joe asked, putting on his

leather bomber jacket. "If you're coming to tell me to get lost, I'm already leaving."

"I want to talk to you."

A puzzled look crossed Joe's face.

Malik motioned for Joe to follow him. When Malik began walking away, he noticed Joe was still standing there. Probably debating whether he should come, Malik figured.

Malik stared at Joe until he reluctantly followed him to his office. Once inside, Malik walked over to the window and looked out. Here was his opportunity to finally get everything off his chest, to tell Joe Johnson exactly what a scuzzball he was—so why did Malik feel nine years old again?

"So, what do you have to say that's so important?" Joe asked, closing Malik's door and folding his arms across his chest. "Because now that I have a full belly, I want to get back to watching football."

Malik turned around and stared at Joe.

"Well? I don't have all day."

"Before I say what I have to say. Why did you come here?"

"To rattle your cage," Joe returned.

"I think you're here because you have no one and you know why that is?"

"I guess you're going to tell me."

"Because you're scum." Malik finally spat the words out.

"What did you say?"

"I said you're scum." Malik said the words louder, so Joe would hear him. "You preyed on my mother, a single, needy woman."

"Your mother was looking for someone to take care of her and her son, and I did that."

"Yeah, you did one helluva job," Malik replied, the anger building. "You put her down and belittled her so you could feel like a man. And when that wasn't good enough, you used your fists to show you were all big and tough. Do you think beating up on a defenseless woman and child makes you a man?"

"I didn't beat you," Joe responded. "You just needed a firm hand."

"A firm hand?" Malik's voice rose. "You call a bloody nose and cracked ribs 'a firm hand'? How about when you fractured my arm? Or knocked me so hard I busted my head against the coffee table and needed ten stitches?" Malik pointed to the fading telltale mark that could still be seen on his forehead, underneath his dreads.

"You were a problem child."

Joe had a comment for every offense that Malik threw at him, and it infuriated Malik. But he didn't stop. He had something to say and he was going to say it.

"Then, if that wasn't enough, you forced my mother to choose between me and you."

"Don't blame me because your mama was weak," Joe replied, and poked Malik's chest with his index finger. "It was her decision to turn her back on you. She's the one you should be angry with, not me."

"A decision that you championed," Malik returned, poking Joe back. "Because of you, I was left in foster care. Because of you, I was left with no one. It's all your fault, Joe. And I'm here to tell you that I blame you. You abused me and my mother for years, but lucky for me the state took me out of the hellhole I was living in. The orphanage wasn't much better, but at least I found people who cared about me. Loved me."

Malik bent down so that he and Joe were eye-to-eye. "I wasn't a bad a child, or unlovable, like you claimed

I was. I am a worthwhile human being and you, Joe Johnson, are nothing but a low-life, wife-beating child abuser who no longer has any hold over me. And do you want to know why?"

"No," Joe said and rolled his eyes, "but I'm sure you're going to tell me."

"Because I am a survivor," Malik continued. "I survived your abuse and I'm still standing."

"Are you finished now?" Joe seemed tired of hearing Malik's tirade.

"I could go on," Malik replied. "But I don't need to. I am free of you, and you no longer have any power over me. So you see, Joe," Malik stood up to his full six-foot-three height, "I'm the one with the last laugh." Malik walked over and opened his office door. "*Now,* you can get out."

"That's it?" Joe asked.

Malik nodded. "Yup, that's it. We're done."

Joe gave him a withering look as he left. Malik knew Joe hadn't understood or cared about a word he'd said, but then again, Malik hadn't done it for Joe, he'd done it for himself.

He returned to the kitchen and dining area with a little more pep in his step. Malik felt like a burden had been lifted off his shoulders and that he could finally breathe again. He had made the first step in getting the monkey off his back.

When Malik strolled back to the table, Peyton breathed a huge sigh of relief. She didn't see any black eyes or detect any broken bones, so that was a good sign. "How'd it go?"

Malik came towards her and kissed her on the cheek. "It went just fine, baby. It went just fine." He took the mashed potato scooper out of her hand.

Peyton squeezed his arm. "I'm glad. I was worried."

"Don't be," Malik replied. "In time, I will get over all the hurt and anger that I have inside, and when I do, I'll be an even better man. Joe will not win." Malik felt Sage and Andrew giving him inquisitive looks, and he gave them an enthusiastic thumbs-ups signal to let them know that everything was going to be all right.

Chapter 17

On Christmas night, Malik and Peyton joined the gang at Quentin's loft, where he was hosting the Christmas party that year.

"Merry Christmas!" Malik said when Quentin opened the door. He gave his friend a hug and a pat on the back with one arm, while juggling gifts in the other.

Malik quickly pushed past him to place all the gifts under the tree. When he saw Dante on the sofa in front of a plasma television, watching highlights of the football game earlier that day, Malik joined him, leaving Peyton at the door.

"See how he forgets about me," Peyton joked as she came inside the loft.

Quentin laughed. "C'mon on in, Peyton." Quentin gave her a hug and kiss on the cheek. "You're looking festive." He regarded her V-neck red sweater, and the black suede pants.

"Thank you, I try," Peyton replied. "Where should I put this?" She held up a honey-baked ham on a platter.

"The kitchen," Quentin said, closing the door. "Avery's in charge tonight."

Peyton found Sage seated at the bar while Avery prepared eggnog in the kitchen.

"Merry Christmas." Peyton kissed Avery on the cheek. "Where do you want this?"

"I'll take it," Avery said, putting the platter on the stove. "And thank you for bringing it. This looks divine, and it will go well with the turkey and stuffing I picked up."

"You mean you didn't cook?" Sage teased from her bar stool.

"Sorry, girl," Avery said, "I'm not domestic."

"Don't worry," Sage replied. "Neither am I. If it wasn't for takeout, I'd starve to death."

"Well, it's time to make a toast," Avery yelled over the roar of the television. She picked up the eggnog tray and walked around the loft making sure each person took a cup.

"Why? What's up?" Dante asked.

Peyton joined Malik on the sofa and he scooted over to make room for her. It surprised him just how much he hated being away from her.

Avery turned down the Christmas music and Quentin hushed the crowd. "Everybody, Avery and I have an announcement to make."

"Ohh, I just love a juicy secret," Sage said, rubbing her hands together in anticipation.

Quentin pulled Avery closer until she was snuggled firmly against his chest. "This morning I asked this beautiful lady to do me the honor of becoming my wife."

"And?" Malik asked.

"I accepted!" Avery held up her left hand, so everyone could see the four-carat, princess-cut diamond ring Quentin had given her.

"Oh my!" Peyton could see the bling all the way from where she was seated.

"That's some rock," Sage commented from the bar, and rose to get a better look.

"You're telling me," Peyton replied. "I'm surprised you can hold your hand up, Avery."

"Don't hate." Sage laughed. "You might be next."

"Hush your mouth," Peyton whispered. She didn't want Malik to freak out hearing the M word. They were in a good place. He was working out his issues in therapy, so Peyton couldn't ask for anything more.

"Congratulations!" Malik rose from the sofa and hugged his best friend. "And you, my dear," he said, kissing Avery's cheek, "are getting a great man."

"Don't I know it," Avery said, and nudged Quentin with her hip.

"I'm so happy for both of you." Sage came forward and hugged Quentin. She'd always had a special fondness for him.

"Thank you, sweetie," Quentin said, and bent down to kiss Sage's forehead.

"All right, everyone," Dante yelled above the crowd, "Let's lift our cups and toast. To Quentin and Avery!"

"To Quentin and Avery!"

While everyone congratulated Quentin, Malik pulled Peyton aside and into the hallway. "Come here," he said, and captured Peyton's lips.

"Mmm...not that I don't like the ardor, but what's gotten into you?" Peyton asked.

"I guess, romance is in the air," Malik replied, caressing her cheek. "Seeing how happy Quentin and Avery are has made me realize just how lucky we are to have found each other. I love you, Peyton Sawyer."

"And I love you, Malik Williams."

Essence **bestselling author**

DONNA HILL

TEMPTATION AND LIES

Book #3 of T.L.C.

Nia Turner's double life as business executive
and undercover operative for covert crime-fighting
organization Tender Loving Care is getting even
more complicated. Steven Long, the man she's seeing,
suspects she's stepping out on him, and Nia's caught
in a web of lies that threatens her relationship. Will
any explanation make up for not telling the truth?

*Available the first week of February 2009
wherever books are sold.*

KIMANI™
ROMANCE

It's a complicated road from friendship to love…

Favorite author

Ann Christopher

Road to Seduction

Eric and Isabella have been best friends forever—until
now. When a road trip unleashes serious sexual tension,
Izzy's afraid falling for playboy Eric is a sure path to
heartache. And Eric's scared of ruining their cherished
friendship. Friends or lovers? They're tempted to find out.

"Christopher has a gift for storytelling."
—*Romantic Times BOOKreviews*

*Available the first week of February 2009
wherever books are sold.*

KIMANI™
ROMANCE

www.kimanipress.com
www.myspace.com/kimanipress   KPAC1030209